BEWITCHED IN BLOOD

HELLHOUND PROTECTORS BOOK 1

JEN KATEMI

Bewitched in Blood (Hellhound Protectors)
Copyright © 2021 Jen Katemi

ISBN-13: 978-0-6451898-1-0

Print Edition
Published by Flourish Books (Jen Katemi)
Cover design by Jacqueline Sweet
Edited by Rainy Kaye

CONTENTS

1

Topaz

I TAKE A DEEP BREATH, resisting the urge to give myself a sharp pinch.

I need to *focus*. The shop is always quiet at the tail end of the day, and it is usually the best time for delicate spell work like this one. My fingers tremble as I smooth down the open page of my notebook and re-read the instructions for what feels like the millionth time.

Stir once clockwise, and twice counter-clockwise, then begin the incantation.

Add a dash of knot bay leaf...

The spell is one of my own making, which is partly what worries me. Not that I'm an untalented spell caster. Far from it. I have enough faith in my own abilities to know I won't inadvertently hurt my customers, but the first step is always the most daunting.

Detective Maewen Jones needs this.

I shake my head, correcting myself. The newly-crowned queen of the Fae Winter Court, half-banshee Maewen, needs this.

I hold up Mae's ring in the fading afternoon light, turning it this way and that, watching the opal shimmer. The trapped flecks of light glisten, and in the very center, my suppression charm still pulses dimly.

Its power has been fading over the past few weeks. Mae called me, exhaustion clouding her voice even over the phone, and told me the urge to wail and cry over every dead body is returning.

She might now be queen alongside her new husband, King Rhodri, but Maewen is determined to maintain her job as a detective in the human realm for as long as she can. That means suppressing her banshee power, at least during the times she is here in the human world and working for the Supernatural Police.

All right. Time to refocus on the page in front of me.

If I can just tweak the magic a little more, then I might be able to make the charm last longer.

Add a drop of mage blood, and weigh it against one raven's feather, until the scales balance...

Great. Now I've lost my place in the notebook.

I close my eyes and breathe quietly for a few seconds, before beginning again.

The truth is, it doesn't matter how many times Mae says it's not on me if anything goes wrong with the spell. If anything happens, I couldn't live with myself.

The new binding spell I've been experimenting with should hold the charm in place; it will at least stop the suppression draining away every few weeks.

If I get it right.

I place the ring on the scales and stand on tiptoe to open my ingredients cabinet. I slide open drawer after drawer and begin to rifle through, in search of my stash of feathers.

I should really get around to labeling all this stuff...

Eventually, I hit upon the correct packet. The feathers are stuffed into the back of the bottom drawer behind several animal skulls. The raven feather is a little bedraggled, but it should still do the job nicely.

Before I can do anything with the feather, my phone rings.

I curse under my breath. Normally I switch my phone to silent while I'm working. I don't know what's wrong with me today—I must have forgotten.

I hover my hand over the phone, hoping the caller will give up. The screen lights up, and I glance down at the name on the screen before I can stop myself. It's my cousin, Amethyst.

Damn. Not someone I can ignore.

The feather flutters onto the table as I pick up the phone instead. "Hey Ammie."

The other end of the line crackles before my cousin's voice comes through. "Topaz. How are you?"

Her tone seems pleasant enough, but I know her well and there is definite tension underlying the words.

I shift from one foot to the other and throw a nervous glance at the door. Admittedly, I am unusually jumpy today, but my protection wards are up. For some reason, though, Amethyst's question sets me on edge.

"I'm fine," I say shortly. The back of my neck prickles, and I rub at it distractedly. "How's it going at the resort? Are you all right?"

We both know she wouldn't be ringing me up out of the blue like this if all is as it should be.

She releases a long, drawn out breath. "I was scrying down by the lake last night and I... I felt something."

My heart thuds beneath my shirt.

Like me—and most of the women in our family tree, for that matter—Amethyst has the gift. Unlike me, however, with my focus on blood magic and spell casting, and my comfortable little spell shop here in the city, her talents lie in *seeing*: journeying beyond our realm and peering via dreams into the machinations of other worlds and realities.

When she's not catering to tourists at her luxury spa resort up in the mountains, that is. Technically, the resort is also mine—I'm a part-owner, as is Amethyst's sister, Sapphire. But Ammie is the one who lives there, and manages it for us all on a daily basis.

I'm far happier remaining down here in the city. And Sapph... well, she lives away from everyone, off on her own somewhere.

"Felt what?" I ask. Even though I'm alone in the shop, my query comes out hushed. I'm not sure I want to know the answer.

"I can't be certain. Some kind of... disturbance, in the ether. Unrest. Something shifting, like a shadow. Have you sensed anything like that recently, Tee?"

"No," I say truthfully. My prickle of unease can hardly be

described in such a way. "I've been feeling a little on edge today, I have to admit, but... it's been quiet here for months. Nothing out of the ordinary."

"Whatever it was felt... familiar, but in a bad way. I don't quite know how to explain it."

A tingle runs down my spine at her words.

He can't be back, surely?

I rub my fingers between my eyebrows, trying to ease the tension, and glance at the half-finished ritual ingredients still scattered across my workspace. "I'm in the middle of casting at the moment, Ammie. Can I call you later, when—"

"Topaz, *please.*" The force in her voice scares me. "I just wanted to check that your wards are up, that's all. Better safe than sorry, right?"

Right.

"They are." I release a sigh, before wandering over to the doorway and running a hand over the carvings there to make doubly certain. "I can reinforce them, here at the shop and also when I get home, if that will make you feel better?"

"Yes. Do that. Please."

"All right." I hadn't actually expected her to insist, but with the wards in place already, it shouldn't take me long to add a little extra protection. I use magic to create a tiny cut across the tip of one finger, and then swipe the resultant droplet of blood over the door. I murmur an incantation, and the wards shimmer reassuringly under my palm as an extra layer of enchantment winds its way through the existing pattern cradling all the entry points. "The wards are strong, Ammie, and I've just boosted them a little. All is fine here."

"No sign of tampering?" Amethyst presses. "Scorch marks, or cracks?"

Scorch marks?

"Um... no." I head over to the desk. "You're starting to freak me out."

"Yeah, well, something's out of kilter. You don't know the ether like I do."

True. I change tack, scrambling around for something to reassure her.

"Hey." I soften my voice, trying for calm. "Last time there was a problem, the Winter Fae took care of it. Whatever it is this time, I'm sure they've got it handled."

"I wish I had your optimism." Amethyst falls quiet. When she finally speaks, her tone is grim. "Just keep your eyes open, Tee. Promise me."

"I promise."

I mean it, too, even though I think she's overreacting. Something older than magic runs between us, a blood kinship that nothing can break.

"Thank you." Amethyst's voice is lighter. It sounds like a weight has been lifted off her shoulders. "Take care of your-self, cousin."

I barely have time to say, *and you*, before she's gone. I shake my head and set down the phone, turning my attention back to the binding spell.

The next couple of hours pass in a haze. Every creak of the floorboards, every muffled street conversation that drifts past my shop window, and every distant police siren makes me tense up.

My mind keeps creeping back to a time and place it doesn't want to revisit in my memories. Last time the ether was 'out of kilter', as Ammie calls it, I almost died. Although my cousins know part of the story, they are not privy to everything. They both know the Winter Fae saved my life—

and that the act caused some kind of imbalance in the etheric energies.

They don't know the Fae used old magic to save me.

Old magic, especially when wielded by Fae warriors, is the most powerful of all the magics. Surely, its protection couldn't have failed now. Could it?

As I begin to pack my tools away, my brass scales tilt sideways, seemingly of their own accord. I reach out and place my finger on the edge of the dish, halting the movement.

That's weird.

The burnished lamp on the wall behind me flickers, the electrically generated flame almost disappearing before surging back to life within the lamp casing. It could be my imagination, but the colors in its stained-glass exterior seem to glow wildly before fading again.

Okay, now I'm really losing it. I roll my eyes at my ridiculous skittishness, and flick the switch, plunging the shop into early evening darkness and slinging my work bag over my shoulder.

One final glance around the shop tells me that everything is as it should be.

No errant spirits or ghosts.

No trace of energy that shouldn't be here.

And definitely no demon lurking in a dark corner, ready to jump out and claim my soul.

Just another ordinary day at the office for this spell-casting gemstone blood witch.

At least, that's the lie I tell myself as I lock up the shop and head for home.

2

I FORGO my usual back-alley shortcuts, taking the longer but more well-lit route through the streets toward my small two-story terrace house on the outskirts of town. I can't shake the feeling that I'm being watched. The trees lining the pavement loom above my head as I scurry along, their spindly branches casting long shadows over the sidewalk. The moon is nothing more than a silvery sliver tonight, peeking through a hazy bank of cloud.

Something scuttles in the shadows nearby. After a heart-clenching moment, I make out a dry leaf tumbling over the pavement.

Its just some goddamn leaves!

Amethyst really got inside my head.

I grit my teeth and pick up the pace. Home is only a couple of blocks from the shop, and I know this city like the back of my hand. Soon enough, I'll be curled up on my sofa with a bowl of pasta, channel surfing.

I'm a grown-ass woman. Just focus on putting one foot in front of the other.

I can't repress a groan of relief the second my front door closes behind me. For a moment, I just stand there, my back against the wood, listening to the quiet ticking of the hall clock and the hum of the refrigerator in the kitchen toward the rear.

Everything is perfectly normal.

I remember my promise to Ammie and take a few minutes to strengthen the wards on doors and windows. No cracks or—heaven forbid—*scorch marks* anywhere to be seen.

Once I have a pot of pasta bubbling away on the stove and the TV on in the background, I close my eyes and let the babbling of a game show host drive out the last vestiges of the day's stresses, leaning back against the counter.

After eating, I sprawl out on the sofa, grabbing the remote.

A sharp *crack* comes from somewhere outside the house.

I tense up.

Great, so this is what it's come to. Freaking out over fallen leaves and twigs snapping underfoot...

I huff with annoyance and turn my attention back to the TV, keeping my eyes fixed on the screen in front of me.

Something rustles outside. If I had to guess, I would say it's coming from the bushes in my pocket-sized back garden.

But I'm not guessing. I'm watching TV instead of acting like a crazy person.

A loud thud, and a muffled whine, coincide with a wallop of power that rushes through my system. *Whoa!* Something just triggered the edge of my ward. I snap off the television, waiting in silence with my breath held. Waiting, and listening intently.

Another stifled whimper breaks the silence. I drop to the floor and crawl over to the window, then peer over the ledge. The curtains are still open, even though night has fallen, as my garden is not overlooked. But tonight, with so little moonlight, the outdoor space is mostly shrouded in darkness.

A large shape takes up space in the middle of my lawn. I squint, trying to make out what it is. From my vantage point, I can only see a vague outline. It looks like some kind of animal: a black dog, perhaps, but if so, it is a very large dog, indeed.

Whatever it is, it's not moving.

Another noise pierces the air. A long, low whine. The poor creature is clearly in pain. It needs to be seen to, and fast.

My stomach twists. Did my ward do that to an innocent animal? I scuttle back from the window, my mind turning over on itself.

I should call someone.

But who? I glance at the clock. It's already past ten p.m. There are emergency vet surgeries open at this hour, but I have no idea where the nearest one might be. I haven't had a familiar since my last cat Alfie passed on two years ago.

I loved him so much I haven't yet had the heart to replace him.

Fucking hell. I might have the heebie-jeebies today, but I can't just leave a poor injured creature out there.

Another awful, wounded noise travels in from the garden.

What if it dies?

Forcing myself to rise, I fumble around on the side table until my fingers close around my protective charm. I slide the charm around my neck and tuck it beneath my shirt. It'll offer scant protection against anything truly heinous, but I feel somewhat better after I put it on. My house wards—powered by my not inconsiderable blood magic—also will provide some protection in the garden, though not as strongly out there.

Probably why the dog is merely injured, and not dead, if it happened to run into them.

I creep away from the window and then grab my jacket and boots from the hallway. I slip them on in the darkness of the kitchen, where my view of the garden isn't much better than it was from the living room.

I open the back door a crack and peer out over the lawn.

The grass is pale and dewy in the scant moonlight. The shape I saw from the window is still nothing more than a nebulous shadow, although I can see the creature's chest heaving up and down in a labored manner. My breath catches as I put a hand on the door handle.

Now or never.

I push open the door, before I can change my mind.

The cold night air makes me shiver, and I tug my jacket more tightly around my body as I sneak across the grass. My breath comes out in white puffs, and the darkness presses menacingly around me.

Shock floods me as I creep close enough for my first proper look at the creature.

I had been so sure it was an animal...

But instead of fur, I'm confronted by a stretch of skin, pale with the cold. *Human* skin.

Curled up on his side, totally motionless, lies a large and very naked man.

My pulse skips frantically. I'm not one of those people who love action and adrenalin. A quiet night in is always my preferred option, and I love routine and order in my day. I'm not equipped to deal with anything out of the ordinary. Not like this.

Maybe he's a shifter.

That would explain the strange animal I was so sure I had seen before. I *did* see fur; I know it. But, shifter or no shifter, I can't leave him out here naked and injured.

I just stand here, dumbstruck, caught between fight or flight with neither instinct winning out.

His chest expands and contracts in short, shallow movements, as if breathing causes him pain.

A dark slick of something glistens on his bare torso. Blood? Or some kind of bruising? Obviously, he ran into my ward, which might account for his lack of consciousness, but it wouldn't account for blood. Perhaps he was trying to get away from an attack of some kind and was injured before he escaped into my back garden?

The sight of his injury galvanizes me into action; I move closer, circling wide in case he makes any sudden movement.

But it's not a trick. The man really is out cold.

"Goddess, please give me strength. And protection, thank you."

Squaring my shoulders, I dig my hands underneath his arms and begin to drag him toward the house.

The going is about as tough as I expect. I'm average height for a woman, but I spend my days pottering around my spell shop, not working out building muscle. And this guy...

He's really freaking big.

The dead weight of a grown man—and a tall, heavily muscled one, at that—coupled with my rising anxiety that he might wake at any moment and ask me what the *hell* I'm doing, makes my progress slow.

When I'm about halfway to my back door, it occurs to me that dragging a strange man into my house might not be the wisest of decisions.

Didn't I promise Amethyst I'd be on my guard?

Yet here I am, only a few hours later, flouting that promise.

I can't leave him out here on the lawn. Whoever—or whatever—attacked him might still be out here, and I'm determined to get the both of us inside before they come back to finish the job.

I don't like using magic unnecessarily, as its use can disrupt the balance of energies nearby. That's a secondary reason for the wards on the shop and my home—they are not only there for protection, but to contain my spell work in a safe environment. But in this case, magic is definitely warranted. He's just too damn heavy.

I cast above the man's unconscious form.

"*Gravitato*," I mutter.

His body lifts from the ground and hovers, his head dropping back slightly to expose the long, tanned line of his throat and causing his inky-black hair to flop down in an artful mess. A flutter of awareness rises up in my belly and I tamp it down.

Wrong time, wrong place, and most definitely, wrong guy.

I take a grip under his arms once again and this time he floats along on a cushion of air until we reach the back door with relative ease.

I figure I'll revive him, treat his wound, and send him on his way. I also want to find out exactly what kind of creature I'm dealing with, and why he ended up on my property.

Needing a hand free to hitch open the door, I release one side of him. He groans a little and I freeze, terrified he'll wake up, but he doesn't. As I steer him through the doorway he remains as unresponsive as ever.

I wave my hand in a casting reversal and his body drops to the tiled floor with a bang.

Oops.

Now I have a naked, injured man on my kitchen floor. Only, he may not be a man at all.

C'mon, Topaz. What's the next step?

I avert my gaze from his naked magnificence, and shrug off my jacket so I can throw it over his lower half in an attempt to provide a little modesty. I race into the next room and snag a cushion off the couch, then hurry back and kneel down to tuck it in beneath his head. Then I take a closer look at the wound. It looks like he was clawed or stabbed, though the edges are a little ragged for a knife. Whatever happened has damaged either his lungs or his ribs.

The wound is no longer seeping much, which is a good sign.

Shifter healing?

I set about rummaging for supplies. Luckily, my kitchen occasionally doubles as a workspace for brewing tinctures and other minor remedies, so I have a separate sink and bench area built-for-purpose in one corner, to keep everything separate from my food.

I grab a swab and a home-made salve from one of the drawers and wipe away the blood before smearing some salve over his injured flesh. My hand shakes, and when I finish applying the salve, I jump back in case he wakes.

He doesn't.

Is he unconscious because of my ward? Or is this a normal shifter thing—going into some kind of deep hibernation-like sleep while the body heals itself? I wish I knew more about shifters.

Witches and shifters are not friends at the best of times. Most shifters actually hate witches and mages. They don't trust our magic. Other than the occasional customer in my spell shop—usually a quick and furtive visit for something simple like a fertility or love charm, I haven't had a lot to do with them.

I gather more ingredients, darting occasional glances at the man, and toward the window where the darkness seems to press in from outside.

I work fast to mix a diagnostic blood spell in a shallow bowl: one that will hopefully tell me what exactly I'm dealing with here. The spell is pretty basic, but I don't have the time or the resources at hand for anything fancy right now.

Finally, I cast my hand over the bowl and focus, adding a push of magic to activate it.

I add the bloody swab from the man into the bowl, then circle back around my kitchen island, squatting down to assess the still-unconscious visitor while I wait for the spell to take effect.

His face is slack, though he is still attractive with strong, even features. He has nice hair: thick and soft, falling in a dark wave over his brow. I take a moment to look over the rest of him. He looks almost peaceful.

That strange sensation flutters in my gut. It feels a little like regret.

Okay, focus. He can't stay here, and I need to figure out who and what this guy is—and what he was doing in my back garden.

I force myself to stand up and head back to the work counter. I rest my elbows on the bench and wait.

And wait.

After what feels like an eternity, the spell begins to take effect. The mixture swirls and shifts, bubbling a little. It glows, flickering into purple, then pale yellow.

Finally, it settles into a dark crimson color, so deep it could almost be black.

Not what I was expecting.

I've been using this diagnostic blood spell for years. I could do it in my sleep.

It has never turned *that* color before.

Frowning, I rummage around in the cabinet above my sink and pull down the heavy tome that once belonged to my mother. The burnished, coppery letters on the front cover bear the title: *A Practical Guide to Home Sorcery.*

The book lands on the counter with a heavy thud. I brush off the dust and scowl, as if the book is responsible for my failure. Then I open it, flicking through. Most of the pages are thick with notes written in a sprawling black ink. Mom's commentary on various spells, and her opinions on the author's instructions, make it frustratingly hard to navigate through the damned thing.

At long last, I land on the section I'm looking for.

Were-panther or wolf shifter? Creature Identification Made Simple.

I skip to the section on diagnostics and scan through the classification markers. Turquoise, cyan, liquid gold... the book cheerfully advises what color the spell turns in the case of wolf shifters, dryads, vampires, or even Fae, but none are a dark crimson. At intervals, I peer at my concoction in case it changes color again. It stubbornly remains the same, no matter how many swear words I throw at it.

Eventually I give up and shove the book away, putting my head in my hands.

When I look up, the naked man is still there. Still unconscious. Still a mystery.

He looks to be breathing more naturally now, and at least he has lost the waxy look in his features. My salve, or his own shifter genes—or perhaps both—are obviously starting to work.

"You know," I say conversationally, into the silence. "You're proving to be *way* more trouble than I expected. What *are* you?"

The man doesn't respond. I let out a sigh and wipe the bowl clean, then fill it with boiling water and leave it to soak in the work sink.

I grab my bag from where I dumped it on the kitchen table earlier and dig through it, pulling out a couple of bandages.

Whatever this guy is, he still bleeds like a human.

"You're lucky I have this stuff on hand," I say, kneeling down beside him and putting a cautious hand on his torso. "Healing spell work can be tricky. Lots of mishaps, workplace injuries, that kind of thing."

As gently as I can, I smooth more salve over his injury and press a clean bandage over the top. His skin feels warm beneath my fingertips, though I suspect that might be his natural state rather than a raised temperature. He has a healthy color back in his cheeks. I lean back on my heels when I'm done, feeling better about his prognosis.

I should get him some clothes.

My closet upstairs in the spare room contains an odd jumble of men's clothes I've accumulated from exes over the years. Not that there have been many of those, but there should be enough choice to at least find him a pair of jeans and t-shirt to fit.

I study his impressive physique and reassess my thoughts. *Maybe.* I don't think I ever dated anyone as superbly muscled as this guy.

I don't want to leave him here alone, but the prospect of reviving him while he is still naked is somehow even more unnerving. In the end, I invoke a spell, holding out my hand to catch the clothing that I've called forth from the cupboard upstairs.

Time to wake the sleeping beauty.

I grip the protection charm around my neck, lay a hand over his forehead, and whisper, "*Felius Surgerei.*"

A pale reddish glow emanates from my palm, bathing him in light. He moans, and his eyelids flicker. As his eyes twitch open, his gaze sharpens, zeroing in on me. His eyes are piercing. Far more piercing than I expected. Even in the low light, they're a deep, intense green.

My pulse races and heat floods my cheeks as that sacred place between my thighs wakes up and lets me know what it thinks.

Holy goddess! This guy is sexy!

Without warning, he reaches out and closes his fingers tight around my wrist.

3

ALARM JOLTS THROUGH ME, replacing the sexual pull.

I try to rip my arm back, but his grip only tightens.

"Who are you?" My heart hammers, rabbit-fast, under my shirt. "*What* are you? And what the hell were you doing in my yard?"

The man blinks a few times, appearing to gather his senses. He stares around the room, then releases my wrist. I jerk away as if I've been stung, shuffling back on my haunches until I reach what I hope is a safe distance.

He half-sits up, leaning on his elbows, looking at me

through a tumble of dark fringe. "Easy. I'm not here to hurt you."

"Yeah, that is not an answer." I'm still reeling from his sudden return to consciousness, even though I'm the one who helped it happen. *Pull it together, Topaz.* He doesn't reach for me again, but I continue to watch him warily.

"What happened out there?" I nod toward the back door. "Who are you?"

"My name's Kyan." He glances sideways at me and then down at himself, running a broad hand over the gauze on his ribs before plucking at my coat, still lying over his hips.

My face heats even more, especially when he lifts the coat to peer beneath.

Is he checking to make sure he's all still in one very large and...err...*impressive* piece? I clear my throat, even though there's no way he can discern my wayward thoughts.

"Wow, you're quite the nurse."

"Kyan *who?*" My snappy tone leaves no doubt about my current mood.

His mouth twitches, but he sobers up the instant he meets my eyes. "Just Kyan. I was sent to find and protect you."

The fear that has lain dormant for months rears up again, like ice shards in my chest. I feel it threatening to choke me. I have to take a couple of deep, calming breaths before I can speak.

"Protect me from what? Or who?" I'm proud of myself for keeping my voice so steady.

"I don't know," he says, spearing me with those arresting eyes.

He sits up properly then, taking a slow look around my kitchen before wincing and rubbing his injured side. "Someone didn't want me to get here alive, that's for sure."

"Did you see who attacked you?" *Other than my ward.* Nervous tension slips into my voice.

He raises one of his eyebrows, before he nods. "I'd just picked the lock on your back gate when two guys jumped me."

I ignore the bit about picking the lock. For now. "Were they...human?"

"Yeah. I should have made easy work of them, only, I ran into your yard to have space to deal with them and then... boom. Nothing. Till I woke up here in your kitchen."

Definitely hit my ward. At least I know it works.

"Okay, well..." I hear the huskiness in my voice, and his gaze snaps back to me. "Put some clothes on."

I shove the pile I called from upstairs into his lap. I glower as a smirk appears on his face.

He clambers to his feet and pulls on a black t-shirt and a pair of dark trousers, then slides his feet into a pair of sturdy boots. As he does so, I stare determinedly at the floor. When he's done, he holds out his hands as if to say, *better?*

Begrudgingly, I have to admit that it *is.* Now that he's clothed, there is less awkwardness when I study his impressive physique. His broad shoulders stretch out the shirt a little more than they should, and the trousers are a touch short in the leg, but the boots seem to fit, and I can bear to look him in the eye now, at least.

I get right down to questions. "What do you mean you don't know *what* you're supposed to protect me from? Who sent you here?"

"My Alpha."

So, I was right. He's definitely a shifter. Not that there is room for much doubt under the bright kitchen lighting. The intensity of his stare and the sheer animal magnetism of the man telegraphs his true nature.

Everything about him makes the hairs on the back of my neck stand up, though I'm not sure if the reaction stems from wariness, or attraction.

"What would a shifter pack want with me?" I demand. "Your kind hate witches and magic."

He gives me a one-shouldered shrug. "Orders are orders."

That is an understatement. From what I know of shifters, which admittedly isn't a lot, they operate under a strict hierarchy. The pack mentality—the drive to follow pack orders—is literally embedded into their genetic code.

We end up standing a few feet apart, eyeing each other up and down. Kyan doesn't make any move to come closer, but I can't fight the urge to fold my arms protectively across my middle.

"You can't just leave it there. You're going to have to do better than that." I jiggle from one foot to the other, unable to stay still. I tilt my chin up at him, my voice hardening. "Or I'm calling the cops. The supes."

Maewen Jones works at the Supernatural Division of the Federal Police, and she has always said she—or one of her team members—is only a phone call away.

"SUDAP?" Slowly, Kyan raises his hands, spreading them out. "No need to call them. I'm no threat to you, Topaz, I swear."

A tingle of something not altogether unpleasant runs through me as he says my name.

Wait a minute. I don't remember telling him my name.

"I'll explain," he adds, hands still spread in a placatory gesture. I can tell he's keeping his voice low, like he's trying not to startle me.

My lips tighten and I narrow my eyes at him.

"Last night, my Alpha sensed a... disturbance. A power

surge beyond the ether. He called me in and told me your name and address, and said I was under strict orders to find you and protect you. He said something is going on and you're likely to be a target. And he said we can't risk losing you."

I frowned. "Who's your Alpha?"

"His name is Burley."

The name doesn't ring any bells. "I don't think I know your Alpha. Why can't he risk losing me? That doesn't even make sense."

"He gives the orders and trusts me to follow them through. So here I am. Ready to protect." A quick grin lights up his face, transforming the intensity into something far more delicious.

I frown, ignoring the butterflies that start up in my belly. "And I'm—what? Just supposed to roll over and play ball?"

His grin disappears at the doggy reference. "Of course. Why wouldn't you accept my help?"

Arrogant son of a bitch.

A thousand cutting retorts crowd the tip of my tongue, but even as I say, "Because I don't know anything about you and your Alpha," there's another flicker of doubt as I consider the full import of his words.

A disturbance beyond the ether.

It's almost exactly what Amethyst said, earlier.

The gateways between the realms are stable. The Fae Winter Court might have given everyone a little wobble there for a while, with the previous King Tryppton losing his mind and his evil queen, Rhodri's mother Rhiannon, threatening the Accord Agreement that keeps all supernatural beings and magic users safe and responsible here in the human world.

But the new King Rhodri, and his half-human, half-banshee detective bride, Maewen, are at the helm of the Winter Court now. Even though Mae spends half her time here in the city working as a senior inspector in SUDAP, things have become remarkably calm.

The thirty-year old Accord Agreement between humans and magical beings is secure, the world I live in is safe, and there's no reason to believe any of that has changed, whatever my cousin thought she felt while scrying.

Kyan's Alpha felt the same thing.

It can't be possible. It can't be.

A wave of dread rushes through me, turning my knees wobbly. If Ammie—and now a random shifter pack—suddenly think I'm a target, that can mean only one thing.

Luthor's back. And he's coming for me.

The tree outside my window shivers as if in portent, and its bare branches trail and tap against the glass.

Part of me always knew this day would come. Now that it might actually be here, I feel like I'm dreaming, like at any second everything—the brightly lit kitchen, the weirdly attractive shifter Kyan, and all these portents coming left, right, and center—will dissolve away, and I'll wake up in my own bed with the morning sunlight streaming in through the window.

"Topaz?"

The sharpness of Kyan's tone startles me out of my stupor. He stares at me with something resembling concern.

"You okay?" His voice is gruff. For the first time, he seems unsure of himself.

I manage a shaky nod. "I'm fine."

The raised eyebrow confirms he doesn't believe me for a second.

He doesn't push the issue further, though. Instead, he

drops into one of the chairs at my small dining table, sprawling out his long legs and crossing them at the ankle.

"Make yourself at home," I mutter, but my sarcastic tone doesn't seem to phase him.

He merely stares at me with those bewitching green eyes as I cross the room toward the door.

"I need to go check my wards."

I feel his eyes burning into my back all the way outside.

Kyan

The witch is jittery, but to her credit she's trying not to show it. I follow her outside, watching as she checks every square inch of her garden's perimeter. She uses some kind of luminosity magic to send all the shadows retreating away.

Impressive.

So was the level of power contained in that damn ward. I pride myself on my inner strength and yet, the second I hit that barrier of hers, I was knocked on my ass as if I were a tiny pup who hadn't yet come into his shifter abilities.

I'm lucky those Otherworld minions didn't follow me in and finish me off while I was lying there in the garden, out of it. I suspect Topaz may have been able to take them on and win, even without me by her side, though.

She isn't what I was expecting when Burley sent me on this mission.

I know why he wants to protect her—the whole pack knows that story by heart—but even so, I thought I'd find a naïve little spell-wielding show pony here at the house, someone who only knows how to infuse a love charm into a bracelet for her customers. Instead, I found a full-strength mage who clearly practises some kind of blood magic, if that red glow surrounding her when I woke up was anything to go by.

Topaz is a mystery, on many levels. She is also one hot-ass woman, with her long dark hair falling casually down past her shoulders, her luscious curves that she doesn't seem to be aware of, and those sea-green eyes that spear me with cool disdain.

Her cool-as-a-cucumber attitude is a front, I'm sure of it. Every so often, I catch a glimpse of more in her features—when she tilts her head a certain way, or when her wide mouth parts and the tip of her tongue creeps out to moisten her lips, or when I catch her checking out my body and trying to hide her response.

She can't hide the scent of desire from one such as me. It is good that she handed me those clothes to dress in, other-wise I may not have been able to hide my body's response to her closeness.

I am not here for pleasure. Not tonight.

Topaz clearly finds nothing of concern in the garden. She re-locks her back gate, waving a hand over the latch in an intricate pattern that I assume means she has just enhanced the security. Then she retraces her steps until she reaches the soft indent in the grass that must mark the spot where I fell.

She squats and places her hand palm-down into the grass. Is that where her big-gun wards begin?

My mouth twists as I realize I must have simply run like a stupid fool straight into them. That accounts for my black-out, though not for how I ended up inside.

She rakes aside the grass with her fingers, exposing a stone marker.

I grunt, and she turns her head to stare at me.

"There's a whole row of these," she says softly. "I buried them when I moved here. If you had arrived with evil intent, the wards would have inflicted far more damage, likely killing you."

She sounds so matter-of-fact. My lips twitch up as I swallow my sudden urge to laugh.

"I am telling you the truth, Topaz. I am here to protect you."

She stares hard, as if trying to see right through me. I try not to let her know it is rather disconcerting. Instead, I stare back, refusing to drop my gaze.

Eventually, she lowers her chin toward the ground.

Submission.

Desire rises so fast I can't stop the tiny growl that erupts from my throat.

She shivers and wraps her arms across her front. Though I have known her scant minutes, already I recognize her need for self-protection.

Overhead, heavy, dark clouds roll across the sky with an almost unnatural speed. The air tastes strangely metallic. I raise my chin and sniff the air—there is a sharp scent on the breeze. Earthy, with the promise of rain. In the distance, a grumble of thunder makes itself heard.

Topaz hurries across toward me and we slip back inside just as fat drops of rain begin to speckle the paving of her patio.

"Do you feel that?" Her voice washes over me, low and soft.

"The coming storm? Of course."

I turn and she is directly behind me. The warmth of her body heats my own. Can she feel this—the thrum of need that fills me when she is so near? The way she takes a step back, ending up right against the now-closed door, tells me she does.

"Don't *do* that."

"Do what?" I blink, distracted by the flare of her pupils as she stares into my eyes.

"Crowd me."

I want to do more than crowd her. Instead, I do as she asks, and step away to give her more room.

She sidles across to the window, trying for composure. There's a crackle of *something* outside—a ripple that permeates the night and lights up the part of my brain that tells me when an Otherworld source is close by.

That isn't the sound of natural lightning, nor thunder.

"Get away from the window. *Now*, Topaz."

She rushes over to stand beside me. Outside, hard rain drums against the ground. A fork of lightning spikes across the sky, flashing sharp light over the garden and revealing a thick fog creeping over the lawn.

"Fog in a storm?" Topaz murmurs, and I fight back the urge to take her into my arms and tell her everything will be okay.

We both know by now it likely won't be.

"We need to leave, Kyan. Please?"

Before I can answer, there's another bolt of lightning and a sharp cracking sound before the fog is cleaved in half.

The fog swirls, re-assembling, until a figure solidifies in the middle of the lawn.

The figure takes a couple of steps forward and stops just before the boundary of the ward. Topaz reaches across and flicks the switch to illuminate her outside lighting, and we both get a clear look at the creature.

It isn't human.

But it *is* wearing the face of a man. Its skin is pale and

bloodless, and its eyes lock onto us through the window-pane. Its expression is devoid of emotion.

Not a vampire.

This creature is one I unfortunately know all too well. The minion of a demon.

Topaz sucks in a deep breath and her fingers scrabble at the charm around her neck. For protection? She closes her hand around it as if drawing comfort from its presence.

Good. We are going to need all the help we can get against this creature.

I reach out to Topaz and draw her in to my side, trying to let her know without words that she is not alone in this.

"You're so warm," she murmurs, and somehow her hand fumbles its way into mine, our fingers entwining in a grip that feels both strange, and yet completely natural. A low growl emanates from my throat as Topaz presses closer against me.

It feels so right to have her here beside me, despite the current circumstances.

The creature outside grins, its lips peeling back to reveal unnaturally sharp teeth. Slowly, it raises one arm and points a long, gnarled finger toward us.

"Topaz Redferne." Although its mouth is moving, I can't shake the feeling that the voice is coming from all sides.

Topaz trembles against me, and I squeeze her hand, trying to impart a sense of assurance. "I won't leave you."

Her laugh is faint and hollow. "You should. If you want to live."

"Have confidence, little witch. You and I together…"

"We can take on the world?"

She has surprised me, yet again. Even in this moment of terror, she is able to call up her sarcasm.

I match her tone, aiming for humor. "Or just a measly little demon wraith."

This time her laughter is genuine, albeit brief.

"It has been a long time," the creature says. "My Master will be pleased to see you, cheater of death."

The expression on its face twists, distorting, and the demonic master lurking beneath the skin shows his ugly face. There is a flash of recognition in the creature's eyes as it stares at me, and then the demon is gone and the wraith is back in control. It begins to chant, bringing up its hands and splaying them flat, as if it is pressing against an invisible barrier.

Is it trying to destroy the wards?

"Can it get through?" I ask the question through clenched teeth, my muscles tensing as I ready for whatever is about to happen next.

"Probably."

Another streak of lightning crackles across the sky, scorching the grass at the demon creature's feet.

"Leave me alone." Topaz's voice is a mere whisper, but the wraith hears her because it shakes its head.

"You escaped my Master once, child."

The wards light up, reddish-gold, and even as I prepare to fend off an attack, I can't help but marvel at the intricacy of Topaz's spell work. So many layers. So detailed and complex.

The lines of magic are burning away, layer by layer, under the efforts of the wraith, until the last protective enchantment fizzles out. She whimpers as the creature takes a step forward, and then another, crossing over the protective perimeter where I became unstuck a short while ago.

The creature laughs with perverse delight when it meets no resistance. "I'm afraid that won't happen twice."

Topaz

THUNDER CRASHES outside and tremors of terror run
through me, but Kyan's hand on my shoulder, wrenching me
around to face him, finally cuts through everything else.

His gaze is wide, flicking wildly between me and the
approaching monster. Calculating the danger. Working out
the odds of different plans of action. But against a demon
wraith, there are no guaranteed plans of action.

I read the scheming in Kyan's eyes, and catch a glimpse

of the shifter within the man—a shifter who is almost anticipating the coming battle. In this moment, I recognize him as a true predator, ready for the hunt. The lick of dark crimson in his gaze is almost as frightening as the approaching demon. I recoil slightly without meaning to. He blinks and the dark light inside him is gone. Instead, it is just Kyan standing there in front of me, his hands firm on my upper arms.

"Guess this is who I'm meant to protect you from." His grin is crooked, and the predatory look returns, though minus the crimson flash this time.

I don't know what kind of shifter he is, but he will be no match for this creature. The wraith will likely enjoy destroying him, to get to me.

"Get back, Kyan," I say. My voice hardly carries over the noise of the storm. "I'll hold the demon off. Go! *Run!*"

"No, I—"

"There isn't time!" I am frantic for him to understand. "If you stay, he'll probably kill us both! Just get out of here!"

I wriggle my upper body out of his grasp and begin to draw inward, gathering the power inside me until I can feel it pulse, red-hot and ready, in my veins.

This is my fight, and mine alone. If the shifter knows what's good for him, he'll take my advice and get out of here as fast as he can.

The back door blasts open, half coming off its hinges. The force knocks me sideways into the kitchen countertop. Cold air from outside rushes in, cooling my hot cheeks. I hold up my arms, palms out, and allow the blood magic free rein. The magic blasts from my body in a stream of red-gold as I aim my attack in the direction of the broken door.

I collapse, bending forward over my knees and heaving

in breaths as I tremble with the effort of releasing so much power all at once.

Most creatures would be reduced to a pile of ash after such an assault.

This being, however—this *demon* wraith—merely steps over the threshold and continues to advance. Its expression is a distorted grin that holds both humor and the promise of death.

So much for my wards.

I raise my hands, drawing in to ready for the next surge of power. The creature stops in the middle of the room and laughs, taunting me. I manage to throw a flaming ball of energy straight at the demon's laughing face. The demon falls backward. I scramble in the direction of the living room nearer the front of the house.

I have no idea where Kyan is. I hope he got away.

My legs shake so hard I can hardly stand upright. I clutch the wall to steady myself.

The assault has weakened me. With every volley, I'm draining my innate power. Spells are one thing, but every witch carries inner power of their own. If my own innate magic drains fully...

I'm not going to make it.

Even if I get to the front door in time, the demon will simply follow me out to the street. It will be on me before I can scream for help, or jump in my car and drive.

As if it has read my mind and wants to demonstrate, the demon takes a giant leap across the room. It throws a jolt of energy at me, knocking me to the floor. My ankle bends unnaturally, and I shriek at the sudden pain. The demon looms over me, taking its time. It is toying with me; I see pleasure in the greedy gaze and the grimace that passes for a grin.

"Delicious little blood witch, all for my Master's plea-sure. You will not die easily, or slowly. Not this time."

The wraith's voice is sibilant, spittle dripping down onto my cheek from its position above me. I try not to gag, wondering if this creature has been given permission to torture me before it delivers my broken body to its master.

I won't go easily. I slash at my forearm with a sharp nail, drawing blood and swiping my fingertips through it. I only need a drop, to boost the blood magic that swirls deep within me. I can blast it out, like I've just done, or I can go direct to the source, so to speak. And the source is much more deadly.

Vaguely, I wonder about Kyan. I wish I'd had the chance to get to know him a little. Find out what that dark crimson color really means. What he *is*—because he sure as heck isn't a wolf.

Movement catches my eye.

Oh, goddess. Kyan didn't run. He's still here.

A shadow flashes across my vision. The demon is knocked sideways and a dining chair clatters to the floor. A dark figure crouches over the downed creature, long limbs and a broad torso pinning the writhing form to the floor with seeming ease.

Kyan.

He still has not shifted, but there's a feral cast to his features and an animal-like growl reverberates through the room. The level of strength he displays is clearly far beyond anything human.

The creature turns his face to me and hisses. "Next time, we'll catch you without the beast."

"Don't count on it." Kyan's voice is not quite human, the words forced out through a series of low and vicious-sounding snarls.

The demon struggles harder and manages to shake off Kyan. As the demon pushes to his feet, Kyan jumps straight onto the creature's back, closing strong hands around its jaw and jerking back its head.

From my position still on the floor, I flick my blood-dipped fingers and fire a sharp blade of magic-heated blood straight up into the demon's exposed throat.

Between the two of us, the demon's head pops right off its shoulders. Kyan staggers backward as the body falls to the floor. He drops the head and it rolls along the ground until it bumps the body. The whole carcass explodes into white-hot flames.

Seconds later there is nothing left of the creature but a pile of ash.

"Well," Kyan says, giving me a strange look. "That was...unexpected."

I scramble to my feet, fighting the urge to throw up. Kyan grabs me around the waist and drags me down the hallway toward the front door.

"It's not dead," he says. "It simply returned to its hell-home and it—or others like it—will be back, for sure."

I know that, of course. *How does he*?

"Keys," he demands. "Where are your car keys, Topaz?"

I have no energy left to argue, or defy, or come up with anything witty at all. I simply point to the earthenware bowl on the side table in the hall. He snatches up the keys, and then a blast of cold air rushes in from outside.

Kyan slams the door behind us, panting. He releases me and I stumble back, taking a half second to collect myself before rushing over to my car. I automatically head to the driver's side, but he points to the other side and slips into the driver's seat himself.

Why I'm letting him boss me around like this is beyond

me at the moment. I'll deal with that issue later. For now, I jump in beside him, almost sobbing with relief, even though I know the car is no safer than anywhere else.

"It got through my wards as if they were butter," I say, and he nods.

"I know." His expression is grim.

"Well, at least it didn't have any hellhound monsters accompanying it, this time."

Kyan's head turns sharply. "This time?"

"Not my first demon rodeo."

"I see." He frowns, before turning away to concentrate on getting the car moving.

Then we are speeding down the road. In the rear-view mirror, I catch a glimpse of my house. From the front it looks as peaceful as always. No sign of what just went on within.

The dark streets rush by in a blur as my mind races, trying to think what to do next. I can't escape the feeling that at any second, another demon will emerge from the shadows.

Clearly, I'm not strong enough to fight.

As if in sympathy, my ankle twinges sharply. I grit my teeth as Kyan bumps over a pothole and his eyes dart over in my direction.

"Sorry," he mutters. He sounds like he means it.

"Inspector Maewen Jones." I struggle to sit upright, clinging to my seat as Kyan hurtles around a bend. "I need to see her. Take me to SUDAP headquarters, please."

If I can get Mae to transport me to the Fae Winter Court, I'll be safe—at least temporarily. Maybe there I can get some answers as to what upset the balance now.

I rattle off the directions to her precinct to Kyan, whose jaw tightens. He keeps his eyes fixed on the road. After a few minutes I let my head loll back against the seat and my mind wanders.

It doesn't take long to realize we're heading in the wrong direction. When I say as much to Kyan, my pulse skittering with irritation as much as panic, he frowns down at the steering wheel.

"I'm taking you to my pack headquarters."

"What?"

"It's my job to keep you safe, and that's what I intend to do. Our pack grounds are the safest place I can think of, right now."

"And I don't get a say in that, I suppose?" I am furious for letting my guard down even for a moment. What the hell was I thinking, actually *trusting* this guy to follow my directions?

Shifters and witches are not friends. Shifters are strong-willed, fierce creatures, answerable only to their pack. They generally abhor witch magic, and they like to play by their own rules. Everyone knows that.

"Afraid not." Kyan's eyes flash over to me again. "Nothing personal. I'm charged with protecting you, and that demon and its puppet wraith will be back. From what I gathered, the creature's master has one hell of a grudge against you."

He poses it almost as a question, and I shudder, remembering the glee in the creature's eyes. "My cousins—Amethyst and Sapphire—"

"Does it know about them?"

"I need to call them just in case. Warn them."

"We can do that, as soon as I get you to my pack lands."

I release a frustrated groan and fall back against my seat,

defeated until I realize I snagged my handbag on the way out. I reach for my phone, only to discover the battery is on one percent. The power snuffs out even as I try to dial.

"Damn it!"

"All right then," he says, his voice softer. "You can use my phone—"

I sit forward quickly.

"As long as you agree to come with me to my pack."

I huff out an annoyed breath as he adds, "Besides, you need to get that ankle seen to." He frowns. "If you walk on it, it'll only get worse."

For a shifter, he's surprisingly thoughtful. A glance at his body language—the relaxed yet alert way he's holding himself compared to earlier—tells me that he's already recovered from his encounter with my wards.

If only I could bounce back so easily.

The silence between us begins to weigh heavily.

"All right."

Not like I have a lot of choice.

He hands across his phone.

I try Amethyst first, but there's no answer. Then I try her spa resort, but of course, it's late and the reception desk is closed. I call Sapphire next and she doesn't pick up either. Worry niggles at me, but Sapph lives way out of the city, nowhere near me or her sister, and I can't imagine my enemy locating her that quickly.

I redial Amethyst and this time, leave a message. "Ammie, I had a visit from an old enemy. I'm okay, but I'm not going to be at home for a bit. Please take care, and check on Sapphire, too. One of you call me when you can, on this number..."

I look inquiringly at Kyan and he rattles off his number, which I repeat before hanging up.

As annoyed as I am with this guy not taking me to SUDAP like I asked, I can't help the grudging respect that fills me when I remember his strength against the demon wraith. My power is not insubstantial, and I couldn't stop the thing. Kyan knocked it right on its ass, with only his human side in evidence.

"Why didn't you shift?"

His expression flickers, and he shrugs. "I didn't need to, did I?"

"Uh, yeah. I...guess not."

He's right. There are few people who go toe-to-toe with a demon wraith and live to tell the tale.

The fact remains that he could have left me on my own back there, but he didn't. No-one would have blamed him for running, especially as we've only just met.

Guess his Alpha must really want to keep me alive. As to why, no idea. I'm not sure I want to find out.

A thrill of nerves runs through me as the lights of the city and surrounding suburbs dwindle around us. We're heading out past the city limits. Kyan shows no sign of slowing; the pack must be located somewhere out in the sticks. Eventually, he turns off the main road onto an unmarked dirt track.

I'm not surprised. Shifters have such heightened senses that few of them enjoy the bright lights and constant noise of the city. Occasionally, a shifter will come by in search of a suppression charm akin to the one I made for Maewen, hoping to dull their supe senses, but it isn't common.

"Are you going to explain why a demon is after you, Topaz?"

My hands twist together in my lap. "It was just a messenger." I don't want to talk about this, but if I don't, I might break apart from the stress of holding everything in.

Besides, I owe Kyan some kind of explanation.

"It was sent by someone else. Someone I met once—a long time ago." I close my eyes, my voice falling to a whisper. "I always knew he'd come back, but I'd managed to convince myself otherwise."

The car is quiet. The only sounds are the consistent rumble of the engine, and overlaying that, Kyan's quiet, steady breathing. For some reason, I'm calmed by the sound, and after a moment, my own breathing steadies, too.

"A higher demon." Kyan's voice is flat; emotionless. It's a statement, not a question.

"A soul collector," I say, opening my eyes. I carefully avoid Kyan's expression, addressing the dashboard as I continue. "By the name of Luthor."

Kyan says nothing, but there's a distinct change in the air. For some reason I can't put my finger on, something passes between us the moment I say the name.

It's a strange sensation—as if he already knew what I was about to say.

Before I can consider the implications, we stop at a gated entrance. Kyan closes his eyes and sits still, before the gates swing open, letting us through.

"How did you...um..."

He grins. "I can communicate telepathically with my pack. Someone hit the buzzer for me."

"Ah." Sort of magic, then, though not quite the same as mine.

As soon as we pass through the gates, Kyan's shoulders relax. Clearly, we are now in his pack territory and the edgy watchfulness that held him tight, eases away.

Me, on the other hand... I swallow hard, glancing out the back window at the gates closing behind us. Nervous butterflies build in my belly. I might have escaped the demon—for now—but what am I heading into? I don't even know Kyan, and I certainly don't know anything about his pack, other than the fact that shifters are well-known to dislike my kind.

"Do you need to let anyone from your coven know where you are?" Kyan asks, driving down an uneven dirt road crowded on both sides by tall trees.

"I don't have a coven, as such. Just my cousins. We call ourselves coven sisters, but it's just the three of us."

"Oh." He shoots a querying look my way, but doesn't question further.

His reticence encourages me to add, "We were foster kids, thrown around between families—some magical, some not. Never got a chance to be part of a coven. So, in the end, we formed our own little gang."

I don't know why I share that with him. It isn't my natural inclination to give out any information at all—especially to a stranger who has coerced me into visiting his shifter pack.

Eventually, the road widens, and we roll to a standstill. Judging by the shapes of dirt bikes and four-wheel-drives on either side of my car, we've reached our destination.

It's impossible to make out too much in the dark. I squint, peering through the windscreen. At least the demon-driven storm has abated and it is no longer raining, though the moon is hidden behind scudding clouds.

A huge wall of wooden slats stands in front of us. I only realize the wall is actually a set of doors when one of them slides opens a crack, and golden light spills out.

I can now make out a little more of my surroundings. The area in front of the building is little more than a scuffed patch of grass, littered with old farm equipment, and in use as a car park of sorts.

Kyan clambers out, then ducks his head back into the car and grins at me, loose and easy. His demeanor has lightened considerably now that we're here.

"C'mon, we don't bite! Except on alternate days."

His eyes twinkle, and mine narrow, which only serves to widen his grin.

"Not funny," I say flatly, shoving open the car door and getting out before I can work up any more anxiety. "Just show me who's in charge around here, okay?"

"Your wish is my command, little witch."

I should admonish him on that term, but the way he says it sounds affectionate rather than derogatory, so for now I let it lie.

Kyan circles around the car and falls into step beside me as we approach the building entrance. My ankle hurts badly and I limp rather than walk, despite my best effort not to show any weakness. He slides a hand under my elbow, providing support without overwhelming me. My heart hammers under my shirt from a whole mix of emotions.

I try to retain my composure on the outside, but I can't shake the feeling that I might be walking straight into the belly of the beast.

The question is, what kind of beast?

5

Kyan

I'VE DONE as Burley asked and brought her here to the pack headquarters. I can sense her fear, though she's trying hard not to show it.

Ordinarily, the scent of terror would incite my hunting instincts to rise, but with Topaz, I feel the opposite. It is all I can do not to drag her into my arms take her back to my place, away from all the prying eyes of my pack mates.

For some reason, the thought of walking in here, to a

den full of shifters all ogling the woman by my side, sets my teeth on edge.

But I have my orders, and at least here, with the particular protections afforded my pack in the human world, Topaz will be safe for tonight.

The din grows louder as we reach the doors. I shoulder it open, gesturing her in with a grin designed to hide my mixed feelings.

"Ladies first."

She takes a deep breath and steps inside.

We are greeted by a sea of faces, some young, some old. Men, women, and even a few children are gathered around small tables and slouched into well-worn couches. Most are clad in a mixture of leather, denim, and plaid.

There's a huge TV mounted on one of the walls, showing a sports game in progress. Right in the middle of the barn is an open-sided fireplace with a stone chimney snaking its way up to the roof. A crackling fire lights the room with a warm glow. A gaggle of kids across the other side is gathered around an air hockey table.

This is where the pack comes to gather and relax. Some of the younger shifters live here in the main building, in the warren of rooms behind this communal area. Others, like me, have our own places, scattered throughout the forest but still on pack land. My home, a two-bed cottage, is about a five-minute walk from here.

Topaz's entrance stops everyone in their tracks. The look that crosses the face of every single person when they catch sight of her isn't exactly friendly, but it isn't hostile either. Murmurs rise through the telepathic link I have with the others and my hackles rise.

I growl back at them through the link and tighten my hold

on Topaz's elbow. She huddles a little closer to me. I'm not sure she even realizes she's doing it, but I enjoy the press of her body against mine, so I don't say anything to dissuade her.

Murmurs break out among the pack.

"Dark crimson again," Topaz mutters.

"What do you mean?"

"Uh, the eyes." She gestures, and I realize two of the nearest male shifters have a tell-tale sheen of color across their vision. This time, I allow my warning growl to surface out loud.

The two men duck their heads and back away, and Topaz releases a small sigh.

Some of the children from the air hockey game skip over, coming right up to openly stare. Topaz seems less daunted by them, so I let go of her elbow and tug at the loose braid of the nearest child. "Give the woman some space, Isabel!"

She shrieks loudly, giggling and dancing back out of reach, before sticking out her tongue at me, unrepentant.

"Where are your manners?" I pretend to scowl, and she giggles again.

"Who doesn't have manners?" Burley's deep voice rumbles through the crowd. He strides toward us.

Topaz's eyes widen as she notes the long, deep scar that carves across my Alpha's cheek and jawline, tailing off halfway down his neck.

A present from a demon and their deadly Shadow's Bane darkness, many years ago.

Burley reaches us, lifting up Isabel and setting her on his shoulder. He turns to Topaz with an easy smile. "Please forgive my daughter. We try not to raise our young like little wildlings, but..." His gaze flickers over to me. "They've picked up some bad habits, I guess. Don't encourage her, Kyan."

"Kyan saved my life," Topaz blurts out, surprising herself as much as me, judging by the look on her face.

Burley raises an eyebrow. She stares back, seeming undaunted by the challenge, at least for a few seconds—which is longer than most others in the pack can stand to stare at the Alpha. Other than me, of course, but then, I'm his second.

She's strong, Kyan. Burley's voice echoes in my head. *Like her mother. She will make someone a worthy mate one day.*

His bellowing laugh echoes out into the room, and I am unsure if he is laughing at my lurch of shock, or just in general. By the knowing look in his eyes, I suspect the former.

I glare back. Is my physical attraction to the witch really that obvious? I thought I was doing a good job of tamping everything down.

The Alpha's mirth floods our telepathic channel until even I have to drop my gaze.

"I am Burley," he says, turning back to Topaz. "I am in charge of this motley crew."

She nods stiffly, wrapping her arms around her middle.

Undaunted, Burley claps a hand down on her shoulder. "Glad to hear Kyan did as he was supposed to do."

He grants me a nod, the laughter gone. "You've done us proud, son."

I incline my head, trying to remain neutral, though pride swells in my chest at the praise.

Topaz clears her throat.

"It's not that I'm ungrateful, but it's not every day a shifter pack sticks out their neck to save a witch. What exactly am I doing here? And..." She frowns up at us both. "Have we met, Mr. Burley?"

The Alpha laughs. "Just Burley. No mister. And, you'll always be welcome here, Topaz. You *and* your two cousins."

Her mouth drops open. "You...you know my family?"

"There is... history."

Topaz looks at me, as if seeking reassurance that she is being given the truth.

I smile noncommittally. It is not up to me to disclose pack business.

Burley seems disinclined to share more at this time, either, though I'm not sure why. He places Isabel back down on the floor and watches her run off toward the air hockey match.

Then he turns back to Topaz. "We can talk about our history, tomorrow. Anything you need—food, rest, medical care—we have it. We'll take care of you. You have my word on that."

After a long moment, in which her gaze flickers toward the group of children around the air hockey table, and then back to me, she nods. "All right. For tonight, at least, I accept your assistance. Thank you."

Topaz

There's a sense of camaraderie here that seems to belie the rumors of aggression and rivalry that dominate the headlines every time a shifter pack makes national news.

That being said...

I may not be a seer like Amethyst, but I am a witch,

nonetheless, with well-developed intuition. And something is *eating* at me about this place.

Wolf shifters—the ones I've met, anyway—are tall and broad, like these guys. There's a feral hunger only half-hidden in their features, again like these shifters. But wolves usually have tawny hair, and their eyes are mostly hazel in hue. Their color according to the blood spell, is a golden-caramel, not dark crimson.

This pack might include a mixture of pale and tawny skin across its members, but all seem to sport the same intense, inky-black hair as Kyan, and none of them have hazel eyes. Everywhere I look, there are deep, vibrant green eyes staring back at me. They are longer limbed and less stocky than wolf shifters tend to be. Their sharp gazes are matched by even sharper grins.

These shifters are definitely not wolves, but they don't look like any other species I can easily identify.

And now, apparently, there is *history* between the shifters and my family.

Kyan leads me through the room, weaving in and out of couches and tables and the people seated around them. He throws out greetings as we go, but I remain stiff, awkwardly favoring my injured ankle as I try in vain to keep up.

As we pass through the space, detail after detail catches my attention, each more puzzling than the last. A long, dark braid snakes over a woman's bare shoulder, showcasing the glint of a silver dagger jewelry piece spiking through the top of her ear.

Shifters can't wear silver... not unless they want to experience third degree burns or poisoning.

It seems rude to stare, or ask her about it. My attention is diverted by another flash of movement, this time from a group of giggling children as they flit past, playing a game of tag. Don't shifter kids have a proper bedtime? I don't have children myself, but if I did, I would certainly have them in bed before now.

An older, brawny man sidles by us. Like Kyan, he's broad-shouldered and handsome, only his dark hair is streaked with a touch of silver at the temples.

Kyan nods at the man. "Dane. Haven't seen you in a while."

"Ky. Been away. Decided to try out the marines. The years went in a flash, I have to admit. Good to be back."

The man disappears into the far reaches of the room, and I shoot a glance at Kyan.

Ky. I like the sound of his nickname in my mind. "Marines?"

His mouth lifts at one corner. "A lot of shifters join the services. The structure and organization, coupled with the excitement and adrenalin, are a drawcard for us."

We reach a small door at the rear of the communal area. He leans against the wood with his hands in his pockets.

"Let's get that ankle seen to, shall we?"

"It's fine," I say automatically.

He raises an eyebrow, obviously unconvinced.

"We have bigger problems than my ankle." I grit my teeth, ignoring the throb of pain that jolts up into my calf when I try and distribute my weight more evenly.

I don't know why I'm being so difficult. Kyan is clearly trying to help me, and I'm blocking him at every turn. His mouth thins at my belligerence, but I stand my ground, feeling mulish.

The truth is... I'm overwhelmed.

This morning I got up and went to work and everything in my life was normal. Tonight, I've been stalked by a demon, whisked away by a sexy stranger, and now I'm standing amidst a bunch of strangers who, despite their bemusing show of kindness, could literally shift into some kind of animal and tear me apart at any moment.

I have no idea who I can trust—other than my cousins who I can't get hold of—and in some ways I don't want to go to them, as I might end up endangering them, too.

There's something about this pack—and in particular, their Alpha, Burley—that is oddly familiar. I try to place his name, to think where I might have heard it before, but I come up empty. I can't put my finger on it. It's like a blank spot in my memory; like trying to recall the details of an elusive dream. The harder I try, the more it slips away.

Everything I have in the city—the life I've worked so hard to build for myself—feels as if it's collapsing like a deck of cards.

Kyan opens the door and holds it for me, irritatingly calm. "At least let me get you some food."

"I already ate at home."

"Well, I'll show you to your room."

I have no comeback for that one. Awkwardly, I brush past him into a large kitchen area. He sucks in a breath as my shoulder catches his torso. I try to ignore the zap of energy that passes between us.

"You must be sick of me by now," I mutter, more to myself than him.

"Sick to death of you," he says dryly, but his quick grin shows he doesn't mean it. He pulls open a cabinet above the countertop and retrieves a first-aid kit. "This thing doesn't see much use—we don't have need of it ourselves, and we don't get many humans passing through these parts."

He opens the kit and riffles through it, taking out a strip of bandage and a splint, before opening the freezer section of the fridge and removing an ice pack. I move my shoulder-bag—which I have, by some miracle, managed to hang on to this whole time—off my shoulder and roll my head, moaning as my tension eases.

When I catch his eye, he's staring at me with a strange expression.

"What?"

He ducks his head, glowering at the floor. "Nothing. Come on, follow me."

Some self-sabotaging part of me wants to challenge him, tease him further. To see what happens to a maybe-wolf shifter when you push him over the edge...

But even in my sleep-deprived state, I know that's a bad idea.

Instead, I limp after him through another door, deeper into the recesses of a building that is proving a lot bigger and grander than it first appears from that barn door entrance. The rooms we pass through are more luxuriously appointed than the kitchen: all warm wooden floors, thick rugs, and large, comfortable-looking furniture.

Finally, Kyan comes to a standstill at the end of a corridor. His hand grazes the small of my back as he guides me with gentle pressure through a final door into a bedroom. Seemingly, he's done with dancing around the issue of whether or not I'll keep following.

The room is much nicer than I expected. There's a patchwork quilt on the bed, a lamp that spreads golden light over the room when Kyan flicks it on, and a thick rug beside the bed. A small ensuite bathroom is situated at the rear. I sink down onto the mattress and smile at the softness.

The smile slides off my face when Kyan drops to his knees on the rug in front of me and puts his hands on either side of my injured leg.

"Hey!" I twist, wrenching my leg away, and he rolls his eyes.

"Really?" He sits back on his heels and looks up at me, frustration burning in his emerald gaze. "You're *hurt*, Topaz. You can't just walk it off!"

"You don't know that," I mutter. Truth is, I do have a spell in my arsenal for healing. I'm just too depleted from the demon fight to use it. "Don't touch me like...like..."

Kyan holds his hands wide and innocuous, just like he did at my house. The corners of his mouth twitch. "Like what?"

My face burns. Infuriated, I push at him with my uninjured foot, aiming for his broad chest.

Before my foot can make contact, he catches it between his hands. My breath stutters to a standstill.

"Shall I let go?"

I open my mouth, but no words come out. He slides his fingers further upward, toward my knee. "Can I remove your boots?"

Slowly, I nod.

He catches the end of the zipper and pulls it down, slow and careful. His eyes never stray from mine.

I don't say anything, but I don't pull away, either.

He pulls the boot free from the arch of my foot and sets it down gently on the floor, followed by my sock. He's silent, watchful, as if whatever this tenuous thing is between us will break if he moves too quickly.

Wordlessly, I offer him my other foot.

He peels off the other boot even more carefully than the first, mindful of my injury. He cradles my sore ankle with his large hands, rolling it gently from one side to the other, before grunting.

"Not broken. Just a sprain. Don't think we'll need the splint, after all."

I watch as he binds the joint with expert precision. His arms are all corded muscle and sinew; his palms rough and calloused. His tenderness surprises me, and perhaps informs my next action.

Either it's that, or I've lost my mind from stress and tiredness.

I hook my free ankle around his side, urging him forward into the space between my thighs.

He slides easily into the gap, as if our bodies are made to fit each other. He lifts my legs up to rest over his shoulders. I gasp as his hands push up under my skirt and bracket my hips on either side.

There's a small part of my brain that screams at me that this is *insane.*

I barely know this man. And, in the hours we've spent together, most of our time has involved running from unfathomable danger.

Maybe it's the adrenalin, or the slight hysteria bubbling inside my chest. Maybe it's the fact that we narrowly escaped with our lives.

Whatever the reason, my head thuds against the mattress as I fall backward, and I moan as his hot mouth presses against the side of my knee. I reach out blindly, my fingers slipping into his hair, clutching hard before I urge him up until his body covers mine.

He settles heavily on top of me. My breath hitches when I feel his hardness against my belly. His fingers glide through my hair, and his hips grind down into mine. I arch my back, increasing the pressure of his rigid flesh against my mound, and another moan escapes at the delicious sensation.

It's been so long. And he feels so damn good...

His gaze is intense as he stares into my eyes. He rocks forward again, deliberately rougher this time, as if testing my response, and I can't help but give him one. My gasp is heartfelt and his grip on my hair tightens.

"Topaz." His voice is a guttural whisper, the sound sending shivers right through my system.

Slowly, he lowers his mouth to mine.

The kiss is unhurried, the connection as easy as breathing. His tongue flicks against mine and I taste his essence for the first time—hints of a deep, dark chocolate, and some kind of spice. The comforting scent of wood smoke rises around us. Pleasure centers between my legs, as if my mouth is somehow intimately connected to my core.

I squeeze my thighs tight around his waist, pressing my heels—injured, uninjured, I don't even care at this point—into the small of his back, encouraging the closeness, sending an unspoken message that I want this. I want this *so bad*.

I don't even care that it's a completely inappropriate time and place.

I whimper as his mouth leaves mine, then arch my head back as his teeth trail along the side of my neck.

"Kyan..." I whisper, raking a hand through his already mussed-up hair. "I..."

Want you, I'm about to add. His head jerks up and his eyes, pupils wide and dark and almost drowning out the green, widen. It's like he's been lost in a fog and he suddenly sees me clearly once again.

"Damn." He pulls back so abruptly I gasp. The warmth and the weight of his body is gone, and I scrabble to straighten my clothing, sitting up on the bed, flushed and confused.

I blink up at him through my tangled hair. It takes a moment to push it out of my face. When I finally get a clear look, I see Kyan still has an erection, and he is breathing as heavily as I am.

So, it isn't that he doesn't want me. Then, why did he stop?

He opens his mouth as if to say something, then closes it again.

Then he turns on his heel and leaves the room, letting the door slam shut behind him.

What the ever-loving hell just happened?

I flop back onto the bed, my mind—and my pulse—still racing. The whole episode can't have taken more than a few minutes, but it feels like hours have passed.

I press my hands to my heated cheeks. I don't know what to feel. Half of me regrets ever coming here with Kyan in the first place, and the other half is lying here, aching and shivery with unfulfilled need pulsing through every inch of my body.

Can this night get any weirder?

My ankle begins to throb, reminding me of all that went on earlier. Kyan assured me that no demon will get past the pack, and I'm inclined to believe him.

The problem is, maybe there are other kinds of danger out there, too. Danger such as the sexy shifter who I suspect is standing guard somewhere outside that door.

I don't know how I know that, but I do. It is as if I feel Kyan's presence, which is both frustrating and comforting at the same time.

My ankle throbs again, and I sigh. There's no way I'm leaving this room for painkillers.

A quick numbing spell helps somewhat, though the

sensation spreads halfway up my calf by accident. Ammie was always better at healing magic than me.

I roll over and press my face into the comforter. I can't think about Amethyst now, or Sapphire, other than to hope they got my message, and that they are both safe and well.

I can't think about Kyan, either. I just need to get some sleep, clear my head, and then hopefully figure out what to do in the morning.

I shuck off my clothes, leaving on my underwear, and crawl under the covers. I reach out and switch off the bedside lamp, laying in the dark while I toss and turn. In spite of the adrenalin of the day—or perhaps because of it —exhaustion crashes into me like a tidal wave.

And yet, I still need to come up with a plan; I can't stay here, around these odd shifters. Not only do I not know who or what they are, but I still have no real idea of their motive for having Kyan bring me here.

Regardless of my doubts, I might be tempted to stay simply for the sense of safety that I undoubtedly feel within these walls—if only the image of those laughing children, skipping around the communal area, did not keep rising in my mind.

These total strangers took me in and offered me shelter without batting an eyelid. And if I stay, my presence here will likely endanger them all.

6

GRAYISH LIGHT FILTERS through the narrow window, rousing me from sleep. When I dig around for my phone on the bedside table, I see that it's still early—not yet seven a.m.

Luckily someone—Kyan most likely—had arranged for a compatible charger in the room. At least I now have communication back. I send a quick text to my cousins to let them know I'm somewhere safe and ask that they call or text me as soon as they can.

Still foggy and disoriented, I stumble into the small bathroom that adjoins the bedroom. I pick up the soap and towels thoughtfully laid out and before long I'm standing under a warm, firm spray of water in the shower.

I close my eyes and, sans coffee, let the water wake me up properly. I'm grateful for the chance to recalibrate after the chaos of yesterday.

I hate chaos.

My inner peace, however, is short-lived. Though there's a tiny part of me that trusts these shifters, I know I can't stay here forever. The pack may have their motives for wanting me safe, but every second I spend here, I'm potentially putting *them* in danger, too.

And there are families here. Children...

The demon's minion did seem to want to wait until Kyan wasn't around, judging by what was said last night, so I can't imagine it would choose to invade pack territory, on its own. But what if it comes back with reinforcements?

After the kindness these people have shown me, the least I can do is get out of their way before the enemy comes knocking.

With a plan cemented in my mind, to sneak away before everyone is up and about, I towel dry my hair and then re-bandage my ankle before dressing. I try not to remember what happened last night when Kyan first put the bandage on for me.

The injury feels a lot better today, though the extra support will be welcome.

I pad around the room, testing out the strapping, and also to appease my curiosity. Is this Kyan's bedroom? Or just a guest room for people like me—strays running from monsters?

My gaze catches on a strange carving in the headboard of the bed. I was too distracted last night to pay much attention to my surroundings. I run my fingers over the wood, frowning.

It's an animal in silhouette, limbs outstretched, running. On either side of the creature are simple etchings that look like dancing flames.

Ordinary enough—shifter packs are heavy on the animal imagery. Why would wolf shifters be any exception?

But... the animal doesn't look like a wolf.

And I'm positive Kyan is not lycanthrope.

A faint noise comes from somewhere outside the room. I tense my spine and straighten, listening hard.

Silence.

I pick up my bag and clutch it to my side. My window of opportunity to sneak away is narrowing with every second.

When I crack open the door and peek out, the hallway is empty.

I try to move as soundlessly as I can, hoping that most of the pack are still asleep—especially given how late they were up last night.

I retrace my steps to the large communal area at the front of the building. It looks different in the daylight, empty and cold. I step around couches, tables, and chairs, careful not to jostle anything.

When I reach the barn door and slide the heavy bolt to the side, I wince at the rasp of metal. Forget shifters. There are *humans* at the city limit probably wondering what the hell that was.

If the pack were asleep before, they're certainly unlikely to be, now.

I shove open the door and rush outside. A fresh breeze hits me, filling my lungs with cool air, and I allow myself a moment to breathe deep as my fingers close around my car keys.

"Bit early for a road-trip, don't you think?"

I jump about a foot in the air and almost drop the keys.

A few feet away, Kyan is leaning, arms folded, against the door of my car, looking for all the world like he's just hanging out and passing the time.

Kyan

I expected her to make a run for it. I read the guilt in her face last night—especially when she looked at the pack kids playing air hockey.

I grin at her shocked look, which quickly turns into a scowl.

"What are you doing out here?" she asks.

"Waiting for you. Obviously."

She tilts her head, studying me, her hair slightly damp and blowing gently in the breeze. She looks clean and fresh, and the urge to take her into my arms and kiss her scowl away almost overtakes me.

I scowl right back at her. "I knew you'd run."

She makes an annoyed noise and strides around the car, holding up the keys and waving them at me. "You're *not* holding me prisoner here."

"You're not a prisoner."

"Good!" She pulls open her car door and slides into the driver's seat.

I wait, breathing heavily and willing my heartbeat to slow before I open the passenger door and lean down. "Just out of interest, where are we going?"

She snorts and puts the key in the ignition. "*We're* not going anywhere. I'm heading off—alone."

"Yeah, that's not going to happen." I glance back at the building. "See, the thing is, it's my duty to protect you—"

"Oh, bloody *hell,* not this again—"

"And if Burley finds out you've taken off without me, I won't be able to show my face round here again. Regardless of whether or not I'm his second."

"That's your problem, not mine." She glares at me.

"I would love to put you over my knee and give you a spanking, little witch."

Fuck. I can't believe those words actually came out of my mouth.

I'm trying to keep things neutral between us, so I can do what I need to without lust or emotion getting in the way. It's the reason I left so abruptly last night—because if I hadn't, we'd have ended up having sex.

I need a clear head to protect her. Every gut instinct I've ever had is telling me that, if Topaz and I have sex, I will *not* be able to keep a clear head.

Her cheeks flush with pink at my declaration, and her delectable mouth drops open as she stares at me.

"You wouldn't dare."

This time I manage to hold back my instinctive *wanna try me* response, giving her a toothy grin instead.

Her fingers squeeze tight on the steering wheel.

"Fine," she says, through clenched teeth. "Get in."

I slide into the seat, adjusting it back to accommodate my long legs.

"This doesn't mean anything," she adds, shifting the car into drive and taking off down the dirt track. "Except that I'd rather not have *you* on my trail along with the demon."

I lean my head against the seat, gazing sidelong at her. Hopefully, my smug grin speaks volumes.

There is silence for the first few miles. Outside the windows, the landscape rolls past, green fields and valleys thick with trees. It has turned into a pleasant, cloudless day, and if it wasn't for the terror of last night, and the strange almost-sexual tension arcing between us, we could almost be out for a simple and relaxing drive in the countryside.

"So," I say, breaking the silence. "Do you have a destination in mind, or...?"

"Of course." She clears her throat, and the rest is delivered in a softer tone. "Amethyst runs a spa resort an hour or two from here. I don't necessarily want to lead trouble to her, but I can't raise her or Sapphire on the phone and I want to double-check they're okay.

"Plus, Ammie's the smart one. She might have some ideas about how I can boost my protections. Save you having to be my constant companion for the rest of your days."

She laughs, but there's an awkwardness to the sound.

Surprise spears through me as I realize I don't hate the idea of having to be around Topaz for longer than expected. That wasn't the case when Burley gave me this task. But now that I've met her, now that I've held her deliciously curved body beneath me, kissed her warm lips...

A lick of need shoots straight to my dick and I move uncomfortably in the seat.

Fuck! Concentrate on the job. Tamp the libido back down.

Silence reigns once again. As the miles of road disappear beneath the wheels, I allow my eyes to close, though I am hyper-aware of every breath, every little move, from Topaz beside me.

When she rolls to a stop, I open my eyes. A gas station. That's good as we both skipped breakfast and I have a shifter's hunger. I need sustenance, and soon.

"Do you want coffee?" she asks.

Her voice is husky. A hot curl of need turns in my stomach. Last night...

We'll have to talk about it sooner or later.

I nod. "Black. No sugar, thanks. And whatever you can find to eat."

Her gaze traverses my face, before she finds the door handle and jumps out.

So, the little witch feels the connection between us, too.

It seems like she's as uncomfortable with it as me.

Topaz

I need coffee—as strong as possible—before I can deal with being in that enclosed space with Kyan for one more second.

I head into the gas station and grab a pack of donuts, my head spinning. There's a sharp prickle beneath my skin again. Now that I've stopped moving, fear rears its head. It surprises me how safe I felt last night at the shifter compound.

Despite the strangeness of the situation, something deep inside me must have known it was okay to fall asleep. Thank goodness.

Not so now. My gaze darts around the space, empty except for an attendant behind a pane of bulletproof glass. Everything is as it should be. Shelves are stacked in neat rows, and generic music hums faintly in the background.

I give myself a mental shake. *Pull it together. Luthor is hardly going to be hiding in the candy aisle.*

Still... I keep one eye on the entrance the whole time I'm in there, and by the time I get back to the car, my jitters are almost out of control.

I hand off a cup of coffee and the donuts to Kyan, who takes them gratefully.

"Want me to drive?"

I shake my head, setting my own cup into the console holder before turning the key in the ignition. I move the car only a few yards, pulling into a parking bay over to the side of the station. Then I turn off the engine and cross my arms, turning to face him.

"I think we need to talk, Kyan."

He tilts his head, looking me up and down. "Well, you did bring me donuts." He flashes one of his grins that I'm beginning to suspect hide a lot more than they show. "What do you want to know?"

"For starters..." I pick up my coffee, needing something to do with my hands. "What the *hell* is up with your pack?"

"That's kind of a broad question," Kyan says. "A little rude, too, if you don't mind me saying."

I ignore his obvious attempt at deflection. "Since when does a wolf shifter pack care about the safety of a witch?" I lean close, until I see a flicker of something crimson behind his eyes. I swallow and move back again. "I'm going with wolf for now, even though I'm positive you're not. But the rest of the question stands. And don't give me some bullshit answer about my family having history with your pack. I need to know more than that, Kyan. My life was *normal*, this time yesterday."

I don't mention the weird carvings in the room I slept in, or the way Kyan's pack members look nothing like any other shifter I've met, wolf or otherwise.

"You *are* owed more, I agree," he says. I'm almost surprised by the sincerity in his voice. It's a far cry from the sardonic tone he seems to have adopted around me, up to now. He takes a couple of bites of donut and swallows before continuing. "Years ago, we had some trouble. I don't really remember it—I was only a kid at the time—but it was bad. Real bad. Our old Alpha—Burley's father—got into this territorial dispute with a pack in the next county. We came here, from... somewhere else, and of course, things got ugly, fast. A new pack moving in... trying to take over land...

"We didn't have the numbers to protect ourselves, and we were facing being wiped out, or having to return to where we came from. Which wasn't an option."

"Where was that?"

He shrugs. "Not relevant. Suffice to say, none of us wanted to go back, and we needed help. The Alpha reached out to the local witch coven."

He glances over at me, and I resist the urge to interrupt. Inside, curiosity burns in my chest. Things must have been seriously bad for a shifter pack to reach out to witches for help.

"There were some who opposed him, of course, but desperate times call for desperate measures, I guess. Most of the coven refused the job, but there were two witches who offered their support. Amber and Lorelei Redferne."

I gape at him, certain that I must have heard wrong.

"Amber Redferne? My *mother*? And... Aunt Lorelei?"

Kyan nods. His eyes are distant; he's clearly recounting a story that's been told many times over. But this is new to me, and the knowledge shocks me. "They ignored the unspoken stand-off between shifters and witches. They helped our pack. Without them, we wouldn't have the territory we do today. I don't even think we'd exist as a pack, anymore."

"Wow." I don't even know what to say. "I...um...never really knew my mom. Or my aunt. They died when I was young."

In truth, that's why I'm so close to my cousins—they are

more like sisters to me. We all grew up together, the three of us shuffled around between relatives and foster homes. Three misfit orphan girls with latent magical powers and no idea how to use them.

"Sorry to hear that. The Redferne name is highly valued by my pack."

"So, what happened?"

"They cast a protection spell over the territory we were claiming as ours," Kyan says. "A strong one. Set up a shield powerful enough to keep out even our most ferocious enemies. That's part of the reason I brought you to pack lands last night—it's the safest place I can think of."

Now that Kyan has shared this information, I think back to the way Burley looked at me—with a kind of pride that seemed so out of place, given I was a stranger to him and his people.

Suddenly, I wish we'd stayed longer. That I'd paid more attention, traced over every inch of the magic embedded in that place. How did I not recognize the feel of the magic as being cast from my own flesh and blood?

I barely have anything of my mother's, save for a few spell books and the protection sigil I wear on the chain around my neck. If only I'd studied those pack wards more closely...

"Topaz?"

"Hmm?" I return my distracted attention to Kyan.

A frown passes over his face, but it's gone before I can really register it. "That's why Burley took such an interest in you. We're shifters; we take care of our own, and we don't *ever* forget a debt. Your mother and her sister saved us. It's the least we can do to protect their blood in return."

He has blindsided me with this story. For a minute or two, we just sit there. The silence isn't awkward this time, however. It's almost comforting, as if I'm sharing a moment of connectedness with a valued friend.

"From everything I've heard, they were remarkable women," Kyan says, breaking the stillness. He spears me with that sincere expression again—the one I don't quite know what to do with. "My memories are kind of vague, but... the witches were very powerful, I do remember that much. Your mother and aunt were unusual magic-wielders, Topaz. They just wanted to help others, regardless of who the others were, where they were from, or what their backgrounds might be."

Grateful tears prick at the back of my eyelids, and I blink hard to hold them in.

"It's lovely to hear that." My lips tighten as I try to maintain control of spiraling emotions. I sniff hard and start the car. "Thank you."

I want to get back on the road and reach Amethyst before I do something stupid, like burst into tears.

I don't know if my cousin will have any answers to our current predicament, but I'm out of ideas at this point. Quite frankly, I need her input.

I just have to hope I'm not bringing danger directly to her door.

7

THE LONG DRIVEWAY leading up to the Aurora Spa & Resort is just as I remember it—peaceful and tranquil. Lined with tall eucalypts and smaller tree ferns, the curved entrance directs visitors toward a large, double-story manor-style building with tall pillars flanking the entrance.

I pull into a marked visitor's car parking spot off to one side. It's late morning now, and the sun beats down warmly as we alight.

Kyan releases a low whistle, squinting up at the grand building before us. "Fancy place your cousin has, here."

I can't disagree with him. The main reception area is situated in a handsome structure with plate glass windows along the front. As we make our way up the flagstone steps between the tall columns, I glance back. The portico is positioned atop a rise, and the view from here is always spectacular. Rolling green grass and manicured garden edging give way to a forest blanket beyond the perimeter of the property. In the distance the cityscape beckons, purple-tinged and hazy.

A tiny strip of sparkling ocean is also visible, right at the edge of the horizon line.

On a day like today, when the weather is clear and bright, this view is worth every cent of the mega-dollars people usually pay to visit the resort.

"She's rightfully very proud of this place," I say. "Actually, so am I. It's...um...part mine as well. And Sapphire's, though she rarely visits."

"Yours? Hmm."

I find myself enjoying the look of surprise on his face.

"Ammie does all the work," I admit. "I'm just a silent partner, really. I much prefer my little shop in the city."

"Well, I didn't expect..." Kyan trails off and I follow his fixed gaze to find out what has caught his eye.

There's a mark on the double-doored entrance. My heart does a strange and almost painful ker-thump. *That's blood.*

It's then that I realize something else.

Where the heck is everyone?

It's not tourist season, yet, but this place is never *totally* empty, even in the off-season. Amethyst and her talented staff have many die-hard clients who come here regularly for the facials, massage, soaps, or simply the scrying spells that we offer on the side.

Except for my car, the car park is completely empty.

Why did I not notice that before?

I crouch down beside the door, my eyes tracking over the blood smeared across the wood.

It's a partial handprint. Bloody finger-prints trail from the door handle, down one of the panels, and end in a couple of drips on one of the flagstones.

"Over here," Kyan says, further along the porch. He points at another small patch of blood speckled over the dark, shiny leaves of one of the potted plants decorating the entry way.

"They got to her already," I mutter, sickness roiling in my gut. "We're too late."

Kyan says nothing, but from the expression on his face, he seems to agree with my assessment.

This is my fault. I turn away from the pity in his expression.

C'mon, Topaz. Pull it together. Think.

I put up my hand, mirroring the handprint on the door, imagining Amethyst doing the same thing. I imagine her grasping the handle, struggling to pull it open.

Sliding her hand downward...

I close my eyes as my fingertips brush the marks left behind.

I'm not a natural at scrying, but maybe I don't need to be. I work with blood in my magic-casting, far more than many other witches. And there's something odd here... something I'm missing...

I smear a droplet of red between my forefinger and thumb, reaching out to sense whatever I can from it. *Not Amethyst's.*

I don't know how I know, other than instinct.

I turn and look to the pot plant once again. Then my

gaze traverses to Kyan, who is crouched over yet another trace of blood on the ground further away.

Whatever happened here, this is not my cousin's blood.

Just then, a memory surfaces, totally out of the blue and so clear it could almost be a vision.

Ammie is sitting on her bed, and I'm slouched on the bed opposite. She kicks her heels against the bedframe, frustrated. In the corner, Sapphire is asleep in her crib, so we have to keep our voices down.

"Ammie, that's not how you play hide and seek!"

"But what about Hansel and Gretel? They did it that way!"

"That's different—they wanted *someone to come find them!" I point at the floor, where Amethyst has left a trail of pebbles leading to the open wardrobe. "If you do that, I'll know exactly where to look for you. That's no fun!"*

"Whatever." Amethyst folds her arms, a stubborn pout on her lips. "I like my way best."

I blink, returning to the present. When Kyan raises his gaze to mine and catches my expression, his brow furrows.

"What is it?"

I hurry over to him. The dark patch of blood on the ground here is bigger than the others, but I ignore the hammering of my heart and try to believe in my own instincts. I rifle through my shoulder bag, pulling out a small vial filled with clear liquid left over from yesterday.

"I should really start making these as travel kits." I shoot a grin at Ky, who simply looks befuddled. It's kind of satisfying to have him on the back foot for once. "Let's see what we're dealing with, shall we?"

I remove the inbuilt swab from the vial and take a sample of the blood, before placing it back into the vial so it sits in the clear liquid. I hold it up to the light. The process will take a few minutes, but I'm impatient. I have to resist the urge to shake the tube—if I do that, I might wreck the sample and have to start all over again.

"Topaz." His gentle hand on my arm pulls me out of my train of thought. "I'm sorry about your cousin. I know it looks like a lot of blood loss, especially for a human, but—"

He falters at the look on my face. "What is it?"

I sit back on my heels, glancing up at the building. We're still alone, with nothing but a warm breeze and a deceptive sense of tranquility to guide us.

"I don't think this is what it looks like."

"Really?" Kyan's tone is skeptical. "Because—and don't take this the wrong way—it looks like an open and shut case to me. Someone was attacked here, and if you can't get hold of your cousin, then chances are, it was her."

He points toward the forest that edges the manicured garden. "Her attackers likely dragged off somewhere... I know it's a lot to take in, but I can scent them. Shifters were here...a particular kind... I know shifters, Topaz, and—"

"Oh yeah?" I raise an eyebrow. "Well, I know my cousin."

Kyan gives me a look. "All right. What are you thinking happened, then?"

I grin at him. "Breadcrumbs."

His eyebrows crinkle together before he shakes his head. "I'm afraid you've lost me."

I point at each of the blood patches in turn. "When Ammie and I were little..."

My mouth quirks up at the memory of Amethyst and me in our little matching dresses, running riot in whatever foster facility we happened to be staying in that month. Poor Sapphire was always running after us, trying to catch up. Unlike these days, when my young cousin has turned out to be possibly the most powerful one of us all.

"We used to play hide and seek," I continue. "Amethyst

was obsessed with the story of Hansel and Gretel. She used to leave little clues—like a trail of breadcrumbs, only whatever she could find, such as pebbles from the garden. She always wanted me to find her. Said it was more fun that way."

"So," Kyan says slowly, frowning down at the blood. "You think she's left us a trail to follow?"

"I do. This is not her blood." I hold up the vial, watching the colors swirl inside, the spell building as it works to identify what type of blood this is. "I'm willing to bet on it."

As if the spell is listening to my words, it shifts rapidly from pale blue, to green, then into orange, before finally settling. I stare at the bottle, my mouth dropping open a little, unable to believe what I'm looking at.

It's the same dark shade of crimson that I got from Kyan.

"What are you doing with the blood?" Kyan peers over. "Let me see."

I start, ducking away from him. "It's nothing," I mumble. "The spell didn't work."

I slide the vial carefully into a side pocket in my bag, zipping it in so it won't break. *Maybe, once we find Amethyst, she can help me identify whatever shifter species this blood belongs to.*

I can barely meet his gaze. *Shifters were here*, he said. *A particular kind...*

Whatever was here, is the same type of shifter as Kyan and his pack.

Am I trusting the wrong person?

Have I brought danger in the form of an unidentified and possibly rogue shifter pack literally to Amethyst's front door?

Is Kyan—my only ally at the present moment—connected to all of this? What if the pack are somehow responsible for Ammie's disappearance? What if the pack are here to hunt the three of us down?

I thought I was running from a demon.

It's all too much to bear. I'm out here in the middle of nowhere, with no one else around, hanging out with a guy who makes my head spin with desire—a guy who also may or may not be a danger to my cousins and me.

On top of that, I'm being hunted by an entity that won't rest until I'm...

I close my eyes, shutting down the rest of that thought.

I don't know what to do.

Kyan

"Topaz?"

Something's wrong. She was obviously already upset over her cousin's whereabouts, but when she shoved that blood vial back in her bag, all the color leached out of her face.

She grits her teeth and turns to me with the fakest smile I've ever seen. "Sorry, I was miles away."

"You were." I step forward and place a hand on her forearm.

She flinches beneath my touch and I quickly remove my hand.

What the hell?

"Are you okay?"

She takes a tiny step back. Away from me. "Yeah, I'm fine. Just, you know, a little worried. Given the circumstances."

"I don't buy that." I keep my voice soft. "See, I can smell

your fear. That's a lot stronger than 'a little bit of worry'. Are you afraid of what's happened to your cousin, Topaz? Or, are you afraid of *me*?"

"No, I—" She swallows the rest of the lie and doesn't finish.

"You don't need to be afraid of me." I step close again, and this time she doesn't move away. "I'm here for *you*, Topaz, whatever happens. I have been charged with protecting you, and that's what I intend to do."

"But what if the enemy turns out to be..." She trails off.

I take a slow, deep breath and let it out in a considered fashion, trying hard to keep my shifter contained.

Does she know? Has she figured it out? Was she about to say, 'one of your own'?

I lower my gaze so she can't see the red flare that I know has just taken over my vision.

Stay focused. Do not let the shifter out.

Not trusting myself to speak, I stare at the ground, fighting for control, only daring to look back up when I finally sense her fear dissipate a touch.

"You could have killed me many times over last night. But you didn't," she says finally. "You saved my life, Kyan, and I thank you. I do trust you—as much as I trust anyone at the moment, which admittedly isn't much at all."

There it is, her trademark self-deprecating laugh. My shifter settles and the tension holding me tight relaxes a notch.

There's an intangible difference in the air when we resume the search. Something has changed; when she looks at me now, I still sense uncertainty, but overlaying that, is an element of trust.

When she offers me her hand, I take it. Her fingers close over mine, and a sense of rightness fills me. "Okay.

Let's follow this damn trail and find your cousin then, shall we?"

I assist her across the grassy slope and around to the rear of the property, toward an area that surrounds a lake. Not that she needs my help, but I'm loathe to let her go.

The pattern of the blood trail leads me to think that Topaz might be right. We likely are following Amethyst's trail of 'breadcrumbs', though why she couldn't have just left a message on Topaz's phone like a normal person is beyond my understanding.

Her cousin sounds kind of weird. But then, I guess I don't have that much experience of witches, so maybe they all do things in an unconventional way.

I use my tracking instincts to assist. As we go, I show Topaz how to read the landscape; how to look for clues that people inadvertently leave in their wake. Eventually, we stop to catch our breaths—not that I need a break, but I think Topaz does. I had forgotten for a while that she actually still has an injured ankle. She leans against the trunk of a nearby tree, her knee bent to take the weight off her ankle as she rests. The sun-drenched bark is against her back, and she stares up at the canopy of leaves above us.

"You're good at this," she says, transferring her attention to me as I turn over a broken twig in the palm of my hand.

"At what?"

"This." She gestures to our forest surroundings. "Tracking."

"Ah. I help out with the younger ones, sometimes. Teach them how to track scents, how to follow someone's trail without getting distracted by other things. When you're a kid, the avalanche on your senses can be..." I break off, frowning down at the twig. "Overwhelming."

She grunts. "Huh. I haven't thought about it before, but

that makes sense to me. I remember the fear I felt as a child —the worry that I'd never be able to control my magical abilities. That I was simply a vessel for the raw, untapped power that surged through me at random moments. Power that only grew, when I hit puberty and then into adulthood."

Maybe she does get it?

"Different abilities, I guess, between supe and witch magic, but that fear of losing control..." I shudder. It still sits with me, that fear, even as a shifter with many adult years under my belt.

"Yes!" She straightens, her gaze intense as she stares at me. "I always thought of my magic as being a potential danger to those around me. Like I might end up hurting someone."

There are so many complex layers to this woman, and they just keep unravelling. The knowledge throws me off-guard. "Guess we have more in common than I thought."

She holds my gaze for only a moment longer, but it feels like an eternity. "I guess we do."

We both stand in silence. It feels like we are on the edge of a precipice, and I still don't know whether or not I want to jump.

I open my mouth to say something, though I'm not sure what, when a patch of darkness at the edge of the treeline catches my eye. "Over there."

We hurry across, crunching over a bed of pine needles toward the base of a tree.

The blood in this spot is darker, like it has been placed with more deliberation than the others. A cursory scan of the area indicates that the trail ends here.

Topaz crouches and peers around the base of the tree trunk, where a mass of roots connects it to the earth.

"Hang on, there's a gap. If I can just..." She gropes around, shoving her hand into a small hole. "Bingo."

I kneel beside her, peering over my shoulder as she pulls out a small silver box.

"Seems you do know your cousin rather well."

"Yes. She can be very annoying."

She runs her fingers around the box lid and murmurs something—an incantation, perhaps? The box springs open to reveal a small scroll inside, neatly tied with a sprig of lavender.

I shake my head as Topaz picks up the scroll and unwraps it.

Witches!

Topaz places the piece of lavender behind her ear in an absent-minded manner. I want to pluck it and then comb my fingers through her tumbling chestnut hair, pulling her in for a kiss.

A low growl begins in my chest, and I swallow it back with difficulty.

Not the time or place.

She reads the note out loud.

"Tee, I'm safe. You'll find me down under the river. You know where. Come as soon as you can. A."

I raise a querying brow. "*Under* the river?"

Topaz exhales shakily. "She's okay. I know where she is."

I grab the scroll from her and read the message for myself. What in hell does it mean?

"Really? I'm not getting anything from this."

"Amethyst is smart. She knew the message might be intercepted." Topaz takes back the piece of parchment and folds it in quarters before slipping it into her jacket pocket. She puts the box into her handbag.

"I gave her the box on her eighteenth birthday. All

this..." She waves a hand. "Ammie just wanted to make sure that the only person who would understand, and the only one who could get to her, would be me."

Impatience narrows my lips. I prefer straight-shooting rather than all this stupid game-playing. "Right, well, let's go find her then."

8

Topaz

A COOL WIND begins to rise as we head back in the direction of the manor house. The sun has disappeared behind scudding gray clouds, sometime between finding the message and leaving the edge of the forest.

I shiver, pulling my jacket more tightly around my body. We're halfway across the grassed area when Kyan stops in his tracks. He grabs my arm, halting my progress, and I jerk to a stop beside him.

"What?" The look on his face sends my heart thudding into overdrive. My annoyance fades, leaving only fear in its wake. "Ky, what's the matter?"

"Did you hear that?" He scans the surrounding area.

I listen carefully, but all I can hear is the rustle of wind in the trees still surrounding us, the crunch of gravel on the winding path beneath my shifting feet, and the sound of cars on the highway in the distance.

"Hear what?"

"Hurry!" His tone is sudden and urgent. He manhandles me in the direction of the car park. I lose my footing and stumble, wrenching my arm out of his grip.

"Don't! My ankle is still a little sore, you know. And, I do have a will of my own! Tell me, please. What did you hear?"

His neck stretches as he lifts his chin. It looks as if he is scenting the breeze.

Then he steps in close to whisper in my ear. "Hellhounds. And they're close."

His proximity shocks me. The heat of his thigh pressed up against mine scatters my attempt to breathe calmly and evenly. Then his pronouncement penetrates my fogged brain and I gasp.

Hellhounds? The hunting dogs of the demon fraternity. The enemy of witches everywhere.

"Are you... sure?"

He releases a light snort. "As sure as I've ever been. There are several of them, I think. They're tracking us—and they have our scent."

"What?"

"Shh..." Kyan drags me further from the edge of the treeline, toward the main building and the car park beyond. This time, I let him. He casts a worried look into the scrubland behind us. Then he focuses back on me. His gaze is intent and watchful, a shimmer of red appearing briefly before he lowers his lids. I realize the shifter beneath the man has surfaced.

"Listen to me." His voice is a low growl. "We won't be able to outrun them."

I gape at him, my mind going blank. Terror pushes everything else aside.

I thought we were only running from demons.

"We can't?" I ask numbly.

"No. Once they're on the scent, they never give up... *ever*. The best I can do is buy you time, try to hold them off while you take the car, find your cousin, and then get as far from here as you can."

"I'm not leaving you," I say firmly. "No way."

"Topaz." He sounds wrecked. "We don't have a choice. This is the only way you'll make it to Amethyst. Trust me. I *know*."

I shake my head. Already, I am drawing on the magic pulsing deep inside me, pulling it forth until its raw power sits just beneath the surface of my skin.

I fan the flame, building the energy and holding it ready in my blood. I will not run off and let someone else take the brunt of what is clearly meant for me.

"How long do we have?" I close my eyes, willing the power to strengthen.

"Not long." Kyan rolls his shoulders, preparing to fight. "Two or three minutes, maybe."

"If there's a chance—*any* chance—we can make it, then we should make a run for it. You and me together." I cast a desperate look toward the front of the property. Kyan can probably cover the distance to my car in a minute or so, but can I?

Unlikely.

I ignore the panic taking hold inside my chest, and this time, it is me who pulls at *his* arm. "Come on, Ky."

A sudden gust of wind whips through the trees around us, and the ground seems to tremble beneath my feet. I don't need the gift of witch magic to know that danger is close by; I can feel it in the tingle along the back of my neck, the itch in my palms, and the shiver across my skin as tiny hairs raise themselves on my arms.

"Topaz, listen to me." Kyan grabs my forearms and shoves his face close to mine. His ragged breath warms my cheek, and his masculine scent rises around me. My heart races when I meet his gaze. His eyes are no longer human. Instead, they are dark crimson, and fierce, and frightening.

His shifter wants out. I can almost see him, prowling, behind Kyan's impassive gaze. Waiting for the opportunity to emerge.

"There is zero chance we will be able to evade them. Promise me you will run as soon as I engage with them."

"No." I don't know why I'm fighting him on this. Something in his expression flickers. Annoyance, and respect. I don't care what he wants. I'm not running off and leaving him to certain death.

"I have magic. I *will* use it." *And my magic is strong enough to be deadly.*

I don't say that last bit out loud, but perhaps he reads it in my face. He releases a long growl, and his eyes flash again. His jaw works, and he takes a couple of deep breaths through his nose. "You are annoyingly stubborn."

Despite my thudding heart and the fear coursing through my veins, I shoot him a quick grin. "I know. Ammie and Sapphire have said that for years. Let's do this, Ky. Together."

I turn and face the trees, waiting. Even I can hear our

trackers now. They're just inside the wooded forest area, close enough that I can make out their panting breaths, the heavy thud of their footfalls. From the way Kyan's head swivels from side to side, I realize that he's right—there must be several of them.

And there are only two of us.

Red, glowing lights appear in a line in front of us. Against the dark leaves, the red dots shine like beacons, watching, waiting.

They're not lights. Terror spikes through me. *They are eyes.*

"Get down," Kyan hisses. "Now!"

I drop to the ground just as a huge black shape bursts out of the undergrowth and lunges straight at my head.

Kyan moves so fast my eyes can't even comprehend it. One moment he is standing watchful beside me, and the next, he is directly in front of me, blocking the creature's leap and twisting his torso to throw the shifter through the air. A roar of rage bursts out of him. I roll over and scramble to my feet, shocked at the speed of the attack.

"Behind you!" he yells.

I whip round, throwing up my hands to create a protective bubble just in time. How did the creature get around us so quickly? How many of these monsters are there?

And they *are* monsters. I've only ever seen an actual hellhound up close, once before—the night Luthor came for my soul, and I only remember snatches of that time.

This one looks like an enormous black dog, but unlike any dog I've ever met, the creature is tall enough—even on four long legs—that its bright red eyes are level with mine. It has a massive head to match the body, and a gaping, sharp-toothed maw dripping with saliva. The jaw is so wide it could easily fit my head inside the cavernous mouth.

It is so close I can count its teeth.

It paces back and forth in front of me, growling in a loud, low voice that sends shivers quaking through me. It is clearly thrown off-guard by my magical force field, but its lip peels back as the growl becomes a purposeful snarl.

My shield, fueled by sheer, panicked instinct, is not going to last much longer. Another hellhound joins the first, glaring at me and growling. Then a third arrives. They stand, waiting for the moment I drop my defenses.

Oh, goddess. Please give me strength.

How do I hold them off?

My outstretched arms begin to shake as the strain of holding the shield kicks in. Where is Kyan now? Is he all right?

Are we both going to die today, on this grassy field behind Amethyst's luxury spa resort?

The random thought pops into my head. *His blood was the same color as the stuff Amethyst left for us.*

Holes begin to form in the rippling shield around me. I try to keep my focus, but I can't hold on much longer.

My arms drop to my sides.

All three creatures launch at me. I scream as a red-hot bolt of light shoots from my body, stunning the hellhounds mid-leap and throwing them back toward the treeline.

The edge of the blast catches Kyan, who was standing over the body of another hound he must have downed only moments earlier. He is knocked back into a nearby tree trunk and slithers to the ground. I stagger across to him. He seems to be uninjured, only dazed.

Thank the goddess he didn't receive the full brunt of my spell.

With a jolt of astonishment, it suddenly occurs to me that he's still in human form.

Why haven't you shifted? I want to scream at him. *What the hell are you waiting for? Shift, and tap in to your true strength.*

The hellhounds stir. My spell has flung them all the way to the edge of the grassed area, but it won't keep them down for good. If anything, all I might have done is piss them off even more.

I hold my chin high and watch them carefully, gathering my power and readying for another blast. There's no time to question Kyan on his motives for not shifting. Nor find out how he disabled a hellhound while still in human form and with no witch magic.

I only have one goal right now, and that is to keep us both alive.

A hound emerges from the shadows, and then another. How many of the damn creatures are there?

The two of them pad forward, impossibly large and so terrifying my breath catches in my throat and won't release. Dead leaves crunch under their huge paws. Their twin gazes of ruby red eyes are unblinkingly focused on me. The movements of this pair are almost leisurely, like they are taking their time on purpose. Toying with their prey, before the final kill.

I sidle backward until I come up against Ky's firm body. He catches me, sending a steadying message. I stretch out my hands, one to each side. I'm ready for the next attack, whichever direction it might come from.

Kyan yells something unintelligible and then he slides out from behind me. He barrels into the leading monster, pushing it into the other beast. The three of them tumble to the ground.

Human against beast—multiple beasts. Surely, he cannot win.

The hellhounds snarl, their teeth and claws flashing as they move. Kyan snarls right back, tangled up in the legs of the larger beast as he wrestles huge paws away from his face. He twists this way and that to evade the snap of those deadly jaws.

A low, rumbling growl from behind me forces my attention away from the hellish fight in front of me.

Oh, no.

Two of the three hellhounds I stunned before are on their feet again. They circle wide, slinking low to the ground.

Stalking me.

They might have recovered... but so have I.

A new fire burns in my veins. They're treating me like prey, moving in a pincer-type formation, trying to box me in so there is nowhere to run. I throw a couple of balls of fire in their path, which slows them down a little. One of the beasts whines and skitters backward, its paws singed and smoking.

But I'm treading water, and they know it. I can't go on like this for much longer. Already I'm weakening, struggling to muster the strength to conjure yet more fire.

Come on, Topaz. Brute strength isn't an option here. So, what's the next move?

In my peripheral vision, I see the fight with Kyan is still in process. One of the beasts slashes through the air; this time, its claws hit home. Kyan yells and clutches at his belly.

Someone screams, high and sharp. It takes me a second to realize the sound has lurched up out of my own throat.

The hellhound nearest to me lunges forward and snaps at my leg. I shoot another fireball at the beast, my mind racing. *Think, think.*

What do I know about hellhounds?

Hellhounds were created in the Otherworld, to serve their demon masters, my brain supplies.

Great. Anything else?

I cobble together every scrap of information gleaned from years of poring over spell books, gathering rumors from the Fae, and who knows where else.

Admittedly, it's not much.

Demons live in the Otherworld. Soul collectors. It is a realm of darkness, where the night never ends...

My eyes snap open. I have an idea.

Summoning my willpower, I mumble the words under my breath. *"Candidus ignis profluentis in sanguinem."*

It takes every ounce of strength left inside me to call forth the remaining fire in my blood. The palms of my hands begin to glow, red-hot and scorching. Bright beams of light burn through my skin. I want to close my eyes against the brightness, but I have to keep them open. I have to see where to aim.

The eyes... those burning, red eyes full of hate and violence and death.

I direct the beams toward every red eye I can see.

The hellhounds whimper. One by one, they drop their heads, twisting their necks, trying to avoid the glare, but it is too late.

I hold my magic steady. Their eyes begin to smolder and singe, burning away until there are only empty sockets left. The beasts claw the ground in agony and rage.

Finally, with unearthly snarls, they disappear one by one into the shadows, their physical forms dissipating until nothing is left, but the broken body of the one Kyan killed.

I collapse to the ground, spent, my magic fizzling out to nothing. I lean on the ground on my hands and knees, gasping for air.

The dead hellhound is directly in front of me. As I lift my face and stare at it, the body disintegrates into ash. Whoever sent them here after me, has called his monstrous servants home.

Every muscle in my body is aching and trembly, though I barely register the pain. There's a dull roaring in my ears and my mind is blank, buzzing with shock and adrenalin. I sit back on my heels, listening closely, but all is quiet. Only my ragged, uneven breaths fill the silence.

Where is Kyan?

The thought crashes into me and I arch around. He is lying face-down in the grass, motionless. I stagger to my feet and lurch over to where he lies. He's unconscious. A pool of blood darkens the ground around him. It seems to be coming from his middle.

I remember that deadly slash of claw. The way Kyan bent forward, clutching at himself, had a terrifying finality to the action.

My throat constricts. He can't die. Not like this.

I drop to my knees and, carefully, turn him over.

His shirt is ripped almost in two, giving me an unimpeded look at his injuries.

His chest and upper abdomen have been clawed wide open. Blood is everywhere. I can even see some of his insides.

I struggle out of my jacket and press it over the wound. In the absence of a hospital operating theater and a whole team of surgeons, he needs healing magic, fast.

This is far worse than anything I have ever tried to heal before, but if I don't try, he'll die for sure. I might not be the best at healing, but right now, I have no choice.

I grit my teeth. I have to try.

"Ky." I lift one of my hands from his stomach, briefly

caressing his cheek. His skin is cold to the touch. "*Kyan*, wake up."

I close my eyes and throw out a desperate prayer to any deity willing to listen.

Don't let him die. Please, don't let him die. Give me the strength I need to fix this.

"Ky, you have to wake up. Don't leave me here alone." I give his shoulder a gentle shake.

The trees shiver around us. Loneliness washes over me like a black tide, even as I gather what little power I have, in readiness for a healing spell.

"Come on. I need you to keep me focused." I allow a tiny laugh to escape, though even I can hear the edge of hysteria in the sound. "You're my protector, remember? Imagine how annoyed Burley will be if you leave me here alone."

Silence is the only answer.

The spark of magic in my blood begins to hum. It is ready to release.

"*Sana aium.*"

Heal him.

The last of my magic drains out of me into Kyan, flowing from my singed hands through the now-ruined jacket bunched over his wound, into his chest and stomach.

This final burst of energy is all I have left, and I give it to him without reservation. He fought for me, when he could have run and saved himself.

The hellhounds didn't want *him*. It was clear that they only wanted me. And yet he stayed, and was injured in the process.

My protector.

I bow my head over him, spent.

"Don't die on me," I whisper, my eyes closing. "Not now. Please."

9

Kyan

WARMTH. Pleasant tingles. A relaxing lethargy.

Sensations creep through my body like someone has injected sparkling wine into my veins.

Not a bad feeling at all.

I lie here, lazily enjoying the warmth, and then memory rushes back in.

The hellhound attack. *Topaz*!

My eyes pop open and I surge up to sitting, only to find

the woman I'm supposed to protect, seated beside me on blood-soaked grass, tears streaking her cheeks.

"*Ky*! You're alive!"

She throws herself on top of me, hugging me fiercely, until I release an involuntary—and very non-sexual —groan.

"Oh, my God. I'm so sorry." She slides back, but I hang onto her. I like the feeling of her body pressed against mine.

But I have to admit...

"It does kinda hurt."

At the same time as I realize I'm the one who spilled all that blood, not her, Topaz's muffled voice rises up from between us. "Be careful. You're injured."

I hold her a few seconds more, reluctant to release her. She's the first human woman who has ever made me feel... the way I feel when she's in my arms.

Eventually, I loosen my hold and she pulls back, laughter and concern and a trace of residual horror still decorating her gaze.

The hellhounds are...*gone*. How did that happen?

My brows come together as I glance around the now-peaceful landscape, trying to get my head around what happened. I managed to kill one—or at least, to send it back to where it came from—and I was fending off a couple of others when one of them got me, and good.

I glance down and wince at all the blood that has leached out of my gut. Half of it is smeared all over Topaz now, too.

I explore a little with my fingers. The wounds that I know must have been pretty close to being fatal, are almost closed over, and though it hurts when I move, the pain is nowhere near where it should be, for the level of injury I received.

"Did you...heal me?" My voice comes out rough and raw. I clear my throat before I try again. "That'll be the second time. Seems I owe you, little witch."

Her smile is tremulous, and her beautiful eyes are almost luminous when she nods. "I think we might be even on that front."

"You're not hurt?"

"Not physically. Though I'm pretty drained, magically speaking."

She looks utterly exhausted, pale and drooping, and I pull her in toward me again, sliding an arm around her waist. She leans her head on my shoulder.

"We need to get away from here," I say, and she nods.

"I know. They'll be back, for sure." She lifts her head to stare into my eyes.

I blink at the wave of emotion that rises up when she does so.

"Are you all right to move, yet?" Her voice is tender, and I almost shake my head, not as an answer to her query, but because I can't believe a witch—and a human one, at that— is showing someone like me any care at all.

"I'm good. Sore, but okay to get out of here. Thanks to you."

I can't help myself. I reach out and wrap a long strand of her hair around my finger. Her cheeks fill with healthy color as she bats me away, but the gesture is half-hearted, and the pink in her face makes her look less fatigued.

"Maybe if you stop diving headfirst into danger at every turn, then I wouldn't have to keep putting you back together. Ever think about that?" She bends her head, rummaging through that seemingly bottomless bag she carts everywhere.

She withdraws a roll of bandage, but her hands tremble. She's not as calm and collected as she'd like to pretend.

I reach out, stilling her movement before she attempts to patch me up.

"Don't do that here. I'm not bleeding anymore, and we should get away first. Drive till we find somewhere random and take cover for the night."

"Somewhere random?" Her voice wobbles, so I keep my tone gentle.

"Somewhere completely unconnected to you or your cousins. Or my pack."

She seems to be on the verge of crying.

I trace her jaw, trying to distract her from tears. "Somewhere to hole up for the night. Both of us can rest and recover, and then we can find your cousin in the morning."

"Okay. That sounds pretty sensible."

I shoot her a grin, trying for humor. "Don't sound so surprised."

She laughs, just a little, but the sound is welcome. It seems she has control of her emotions once again.

We help each other stagger to our feet, and it takes twice as long to get back to the car as it did on the outward journey.

"I'll drive," I start, but as pain lashes through my middle and I wince, she raises a brow.

"No way. I'm driving, shifter man."

Seems I'm maybe not quite as healed as I thought.

"Yeah, okay," I say, and we climb into the car. We take off back down the driveway and out onto the highway. At this time of the evening, when dusk is falling, there's a bit more traffic than there was earlier, but not much.

She drives aimlessly, until we pass a small sign advertising a vacancy for a bed-and-breakfast facility.

"This one do?" She slants a quick gaze at me, and I nod.

"Sure. As long as it isn't owned or run by you or one of your cousins."

"Nope."

"All good then."

She turns in to the unmade road and passes a house with lights blazing at the windows. Further up the road, tucked well out of sight of the house, are four cabins, all dark and silent and overlooking a still, silent pond.

A light mist has fallen over the water. It's nothing like the demonic fog at Topaz's house last night, but it sends a ripple of unease through my body.

We need a place to rest and recoup our energy. Neither of us are fit to drive far right now, and I would be next-to-useless in a battle. We need to regain our strength before we can move on.

This place seems as good as any for that purpose.

Clearly, there is no one in residence in any of the cabins at the moment, which is a good start.

"Park the car behind that last cabin, well into the tree-line," I say, and Topaz complies. When she turns off the engine, the silence builds, until she looks down at her blood-soaked shirt and sucks in a quick breath.

"Damn. I don't even think I have enough magic in reserve to clean this—"

"You won't need to, at least tonight. I'm very good at break-and-enter, you know."

Her eyes widen. "But what if they've been rented for the night and the guests are simply out for dinner or something?"

"I'll double check." I climb out of the car and gingerly shift several fallen branches to camouflage the vehicle, mindful of the pain of my still-healing wounds. Then I wander over to each of the four cabins in turn, sniffing the air for a scent of any recent habitation.

There's nothing except cleaning product and dust.

I return to Topaz, who waits with a look of trepidation on her face. The trepidation turns to relief as I shake my head.

"No one's been here for at least a couple of days, and I'd say it's far too late in the evening for any check-ins."

I hold out my hand, and after a second's hesitation, she steps forward to take it. As soon as our skin touches, a zing of energy shoots up my arm. The tiny hitch in her breath confirms that she feels the connection, too.

"You really think we'll be safe here tonight, Ky?"

I love it when she uses the shortened version of my name. It sounds good, coming from her.

"As long as we're gone by daybreak, then yes. I do."

"All right then. I've never broken in anywhere before, so this will be a first for me."

There's a note in her voice that almost sounds like excitement.

My respect for this woman grows. Topaz is one of the most resilient humans I've ever met—magical or otherwise. Even after all we've been through in the past twenty-four hours or so, her spirit remains unbroken.

As we climb the small set of steps onto the front porch, I acknowledge that this whole situation with Topaz—the fact that she is beginning to trust me, and the clear evidence of our mutual desire—is also a first for me.

She watches while I work on the door. It only takes a minute or so before I hear the lock click, and the door swings open.

I head in first, checking out the space. It is small, but

comfortable. There's a living area with a kitchenette, and one bedroom with a bathroom leading off it.

I head back to the entrance and gesture for Topaz to come inside. She stands at the threshold, her hands clenched by her side and an unreadable expression on her face.

"It's safe, Topaz. I promise. There's even crackers, fruit, and wine on the bench and cheese in the little fridge. We can have a midnight snack later. It's perfect! Come on in."

She releases a small laugh, and finally enters the cabin. "Will you protect me if I can't keep my eyes open?"

She dumps her bag on the sofa and grips the back of one of the sofa chairs. Once again, she seems far too pale.

"Are you okay... hey. *Topaz*?"

I jump forward and catch her as she tilts sideways, sweeping her up into my arms. I grunt at the ripple of pain in my gut area, but I'm determined not to drop her.

"So sleepy," she mumbles, tucking her face into my shoulder. "From the magic draining out. I think."

A wave of longing washes over me as her delicate perfume wafts up into my nostrils. I try to tamp the feeling back down.

Not the time for anything like that.

"Let's get you to bed, then," I murmur. I carry her through to the bedroom and lay her gently on the bed. She has enough presence of mind to wriggle around and assist as I work the cover out from beneath her, then she yawns and snuggles in as I remove her boots and lay the cover back over the top of her.

I draw the curtains shut, and then switch on one of the bedside lamps. It casts a gentle golden glow over the room.

"I'll watch over you," I say, and she smiles dreamily.

"I know you will."

Then she's gone, fast asleep, as I sink into the armchair in the corner of the room and stretch out my legs in front of me.

I have no idea what tomorrow will bring, nor how I will make good on my promise to keep her safe beyond the here and now.

But for tonight at least, I will not let any enemies cross the threshold of this cottage. I will do my utmost to let her rest without fear of monsters keeping both of us awake.

10

Topaz

I WAKE to the sight of Kyan and his long limbs half-pretzeled into the corner armchair. He looks terribly uncomfortable, and a wave of guilt washes over me.

"Hell, Ky. You should have taken the bed beside me. You're the injured one!"

He shakes his head.

My cheeks flush with heat. I know exactly what he's alluding to, without him having to utter a word. There's something happening between us, and if we were both stretched out side by side on this bed...

Maybe he made the right call, after all.

When I sit up, dizziness hits me like a brick wall, and I have to wait a second for it to pass. It leaves a headache residue, and I groan and press a hand to my forehead. "How long was I out?"

"About three hours," Kyan says. "You sure needed it."

At some point while I was asleep, he must have been back out to the other room. My bag is on the floor next to the bed, and a plate full of cheese, crackers, nuts, and some wedges of apple and orange, sits on the bedside table beside a bottle of water, and a glass of red wine.

My stomach rumbles as I snap open the water bottle and drink, then attack the food. It feels like forever ago that I ate.

"Fancy supper," I mumble, between bites. At last I'm sated. "Sorry. Didn't realize how hungry I was."

"Don't be sorry. I couldn't even wait for you to wake up. A shifter cannot live on one serving of donuts and coffee per day. I ate all the packaged meats in the refrigerator. Hope you don't mind?"

I wrinkle my nose. "I don't eat meat."

"Ah. Well, that works, then, as I love it."

He bends to one side, and retrieves a half-drunk glass of red wine from the floor beside his chair.

I snag my glass and raise it. "Here's to..." *Us*, I almost say, but that sounds too intimate. "To a better day tomorrow," I finish lamely, before taking a sip.

One corner of his mouth curves up. "I'll drink to that."

He does, before leaning forward, clasping the wine glass loosely, and resting his forearms on his knees.

When he winces, all the memories come back to me in a rush.

"You're still hurting." I look him over with a more critical eye. His posture is casual, loose, but he's sitting awkwardly, slightly hunched. "You should have said."

"I'm good."

"No, you're not." I flip aside the bed covers and climb out, kneeling down in front of him. "Why didn't you shift? During the attack, or after? Doesn't that help the healing process?"

"It does. But..." He shrugs and stares somewhere above my head. Almost as if he doesn't want to meet my gaze. "I didn't want to."

"Fair enough." He allows me to take his glass and put it aside. "Do you mind... taking this off?" I pluck at his torn and blood-covered shirt.

"You planning to ravish me, then?"

There's an instant ache between my legs and my nipples pebble into hardness.

"No." I dip my head, allowing my hair to drop down and hide my expression. "I just want to...err... check your wounds."

He reaches out one long finger and lifts my chin, forcing me to meet his gaze.

Desire is rampant in his eyes, but his face is unnaturally pale and his breathing is shallower than it should be.

"My wound is healing nicely. Just need a few more hours and I'll be as good as new."

I frown, the rising lust within me tamped down. "Let me help the process along, a little bit."

"You need to rest, Topaz."

I tut and reach for my bag. "Not this again. I'm fine, now that I've slept."

"Hey, you know I'm right."

"No. *I'm* right." I let out a huff of relief when my fingers close around a small jar filled with aniseed root in my bag. "Here, bite down on a piece of this. It's charmed. It'll help with any residual pain."

He raises an eyebrow when I pass him a piece of the root, but he does as I say without complaining. After some more rummaging, I realize I'm running low on medicinal supplies. All those diagnostic spells, and now healing, which definitely is not my strong suit...

I come across a small jar of the facial cleanser Amethyst created, that we use in the spa treatments. She gave some to me last time I was out visiting, and I must have put it in my bag and forgotten about it. Till now.

Excellent.

While I might be average at healing, Amethyst's skills in that area are a whole lot stronger than mine. There's a reason our resort is the most popular spa facility this side of the bay area; everything she uses contains a little something extra.

I grin as I hold up the jar. The contents shimmer and swirl in the light cast by the lamp.

It's not perfect, but it'll do in a pinch. And this is one hell of a pinch.

I hurry into the bathroom and snag a couple of towels. It's time for some improvising.

When I return, Kyan has removed his shirt. I stop dead at the sight of his hard, muscled body. There isn't an ounce of fat anywhere on him. He looks so fit and incredibly sexy. Butterflies start up in my belly, and wander south, all the way down to that sacred space between my legs.

I squeeze my legs tight, trying to control my urges, but that only heightens the desire.

I clear my throat, focusing on the ragged gash that runs

from his right collarbone all the way down across his chest and upper abdomen, tapering off below his ribs on the left.

The flesh has knitted nicely, and it is no longer bleeding at all, but the wound is red and raw.

He needs to rest. Not... I swallow hard. Not anything else.

I drop down in front of him, and one of his hands closes around my wrist. "Wait. I..." He takes a deep breath and a small frown appears as his brows draw together. "Thank you."

I get the impression he's not used to receiving help from anyone. I'm quite sure he has never had a *witch* fussing over him. I grin up at him, trying to let him know that it's okay for everyone to accept support when they need it. "No problem."

The sudden vulnerability in his expression is my undoing. Something catches inside my chest, and before I can stop myself, I reach up and smooth back some of the wayward hair that has dropped down into his eyes.

He turns his head and presses a kiss to my palm.

I hitch a breath and hold it, before pulling back my hand.

"Let's see what we can do with this," I say, but my voice comes out all husky and low, not sounding like my usual light tone at all.

He grunts as I explore the wound. Heat under my fingertips confirms there is still a lot going on beneath the surface.

"You shouldn't have let me sleep so long," I murmur.

He throws a crooked grin in my direction. "You needed it."

I don't know what to say to that, because he's right. My powers aren't yet fully restored, but I feel a whole lot better than I did when we staggered through the cabin door earlier.

I open the jar of cleanser and begin to treat his injury. After a moment, I reach into my bag and snag some powdered arrowroot which I add to the ointment. I focus on getting the concoction just the right consistency before I continue to apply it to his chest in gentle circular movements.

His eyes remain fixed on me as I work.

"You mentioned yesterday that you're not too good at healing. I beg to differ, Topaz. You have very restful... hands."

"Um... thanks." This situation is suddenly far more intimate than I planned. My face heats, but I don't stop what I'm doing. His muscles beneath my fingertips are firm and undulating and his skin is warm and silken. Soft and hard, all in one delicious package.

My breathing becomes uneven.

Concentrate on the task.

"What would I do without you, little witch?" He leans into my touch, and at last the tincture on his skin begins to glow a little brighter. It's working.

"Only the goddess knows. At the rate you're going, I'm surprised you've survived this long without me."

He releases a bark of laughter that quickly turns into a hiss. The tincture glows brighter as the magic draws damaged tissue together, burning out anything that isn't as it should be.

"What did you do?"

I glance at him as I put the ingredients back into my bag. "Boosted the restorative magic in Amethyst's facial cleanser with a little extra embellishment of my own. She uses it to give her clients rejuvenated skin. I figured a little spelled powder might help to actually *repair* yours. And the organs beneath."

He stares at me with something like awe. "That makes sense," he says eventually. "And I feel much better already, so whatever you did, worked very well."

I look away, embarrassed.

"Hey." His fingers brush the edge of my jaw. When I look up, he slides both of his hands into my hair, cupping my head and forcing my gaze to meet his. "I have to say, you're nothing like what I was expecting when Burley sent me to find you."

He chuckles in a soft, low way that makes me ache in all my womanly places.

His hands slide down over my shoulders and reach my waist. He grips hard, encouraging me closer. Emboldened, I let him draw me in, fitting neatly in the space between his open thighs. I revel in his proximity, his heat.

"I know the feeling," I murmur.

Now that's an understatement.

It's been a long time since I've been with a man in a sexual way. The past couple of days have been more than crazy, but for some reason, with Ky, it is as if I cannot help myself. When it comes to this shifter, my body doesn't want to accept the word *no*.

His fingers tighten as if reflexively, and I kneel up until my mound grinds against his hardening flesh. It is all I can do not to let out a heartfelt moan.

He grips me under the arms, lifting me up until I straddle his lap. I settle against him, rocking my hips and enjoying the pressure against my clit.

"You're still recovering," I whisper, and he laughs, shaking us both.

"Not anymore. Thanks to you." Then his face turns serious. "You're beautiful, Topaz. I've never met anyone like you before."

His hands cradle my hips, encouraging my gentle rocking. His eyes burn with intensity. The low tenor of his voice vibrates through my body, sending shivers down my spine.

"When you walk into a room, I have trouble concentrating on anything else." He raises one hand and traces up over my ribs to tease at my already hard nipples. First the right, then the left.

This time, I can't hold the moan inside.

The sound is followed by a low growl from Kyan. He bends his head and brushes his lips teasingly against the pulse point in my neck.

"Ever since I laid eyes on you, I feel like I'm barely holding it together."

The desire that washes through my veins is so potent every part of me starts to shake. "I know what you mean. And I think you should stop trying to hold it together, Ky." I arch against him, unable to stop my actions and reactions when it comes to this man. "Do whatever you want with me, before you drive me insane."

11

Kyan

HER WORDS REMOVE the last vestiges of my control.

We tear frantically at each other's clothes and throw them aside. She climbs back onto my lap, arching her back and pushing those delicious, pink-tipped breasts straight into my face. Electricity runs through me as I duck my head and accept her offering, taking first one and then the other breast into my mouth.

I suck at the already hard nipples, flicking them and circling with my tongue, drawing the peaks out even more.

My reward is the groan that rolls up out of her throat, as if she's trying to contain her desire and it proves too much.

God, this woman is so sexy.

She tastes sweet and spicy all at once. I lick at her skin, learning her scent and her taste and finding the mix a heady one.

"You smell divine, Topaz." My voice is raspy and rough. She rides the swell of my cock with an undulating movement that creates shudders through my system. Her scent continues to rise around us. Her fingers are in my hair, grasping and holding on, as I buck beneath her. At this rate, we won't last long.

My breathing is as uneven as hers, and I try to slow down. "Wait, Topaz. Slower...ah, God, that feels fucking good."

She reaches down between our bodies and the swish of her fingers as they brush my erection is an aphrodisiac all its own.

I quickly stand, bringing her up with me before I dump her down on the bed.

She sprawls, arms akimbo, her dark hair sprawled across the bedcover, looking like a siren about to entice a sailor to his doom.

I don't care. I want her, more than I've ever wanted anyone.

Quickly, I join her on the bed, kneeling beside her, staring down. She reaches out to clasp my cock in her hand.

I shudder and thrust my hips, enjoying the heat of her grip.

I am so ready for her. My cock is almost vertical.

"I want you inside of me, Ky. Now."

I want that too, but I want to enjoy this moment a little longer, before I sink my hardness into her body and we lose ourselves completely.

"Soon, my little witch. But not yet."

"I love it when you call me that." Her voice is husky. "I hated it at first, but now..."

"Sexy little witch."

I lie down beside her, tracing patterns over her stomach and ribs and enjoying the goose bumps that rise in the wake of my touch.

I should tell her the truth before we take this any further.

The realization stays my exploring fingers.

I *need* to tell her the truth.

I open my mouth to explain why I didn't shift before; why I held so goddamn hard onto my control that I almost lost her life—and my own—in the process.

But she pushes at me, forcing me onto my back, and then leans down to take my erection into her mouth.

All rational thought disappears out of my head and all I can do is buck and groan beneath her ministrations.

Topaz

One of his hands tangles in my hair, gently guiding my head as I slide my mouth up and down his flesh and cup my hand around his balls. The sounds of pleasure erupting from him somewhere above push my own desire into overdrive.

Wetness pools between my legs and the ache that has been echoing within me since last night at Kyan's pack headquarters is back. Only this time, the need is amplified a thousand-fold.

This feels so right. It's as if I've been waiting for Kyan for such a long time. I can't believe we only met a couple of days ago.

I'm so close to climax, but I need to hold on. I want him inside me when I come.

Abruptly he stops my action, and then hauls me up until I lay beside him. His skin is warm where it touches mine, and his erection squashed between our bellies is hot and hard.

His wound is completely closed over and no longer red-raw, though there is still a jagged scar running across his torso. Gently I reach out and run my finger along the line.

He shivers, but I can tell from the flare in his eyes that the reaction is born of desire, not pain.

His gaze rakes across my body, hungry and glittering. I don't think it's my imagination; there's a hint of shifter in his gaze. Something not quite human, intensely focused on me.

I resist the urge to cover myself and stare back with a mix of anxiety and anticipation.

"It's been... a while," I manage.

His grin is my undoing. Heat rushes into my cheeks.

"You're doing okay so far."

"Just okay?"

He smooths a wayward lock of hair off my face. "Pretty damn fantastic, actually."

Then he leans in to kiss me, and I lose all ability to think. I can only feel as his lips and mouth take mine in a way that makes me forget everything.

Except pleasure.

He tastes divine—like some kind of spicy and exotic scent that is an aphrodisiac all its own. His tongue teases a response from me, in a sensual dance, and I open my mouth fully to let him in.

His hands explore everywhere—up my sides, across the swell of my breasts, down my stomach to cup my mound and circle my clit seductively. Then he slips a finger along my seam, finding my channel entrance and grunting as he discovers my readiness.

"So wet, little witch. You're ready for me, then?"

"More than ready, shifter man."

Somehow, I end up beneath him. He holds himself up on his elbows as his erection glides between my legs.

I gasp and wriggle, too impatient to wait.

"Do you want me to use protection?" he asks in a rough growl. "I have something in my wallet if—"

"No. I have magic." I wave my hand, indicating the ring on my left forefinger. The topaz stone contains a charm that will protect against unwanted consequences. Not that it has had much use in recent times.

He kisses me again, a slow and seductive connection, that continues as he positions himself properly between my legs and slides his cock inside me.

I moan at the exquisite sensation of fullness, hooking my feet around his hips to rest on his ass. I slide my arms around his midriff and his low growl reverberates against my chest.

Everything about him drives me crazy: the slick heat of his tongue against mine, the firm, possessive touch of his broad fingers, the way he hisses between his teeth when I squeeze my inner muscles and clench around his cock.

He breaks off our kiss and one of his hands slides up and tangles in my hair. He forces my head back, exposing my throat, and his teeth drag along my pulse point.

"God, Topaz," he groans against my skin. "You're so tight and hot. You feel fucking fantastic."

"Stop teasing." I jerk my pelvis to increase the pressure against my clit. "Just go hard. *Now*, please."

He begins to pump his hips. The heat builds, deep inside, and with every thrust, I draw closer to the edge. I shiver and writhe beneath him as his driving movements become more frenzied. He fucks me in earnest, with short sharp thrusts that leave me helpless to do anything but cry out in wordless noises as he grunts and growls with every assault on my core.

When his mouth closes around one of my nipples and he grazes me with his teeth, I arch up and clench my jaw to hold in the scream that threatens to burst out of me.

The orgasm crashes over me without warning. I ride it out, shuddering senselessly beneath him. He doesn't let up, merciless with his attentions until I push him off my breasts, gasping and spent.

"My turn," I say, and force him over, onto his back. I roll with him, managing to keep him seated deep inside me as I rise up until I'm straddling his hips.

His eyes are narrowed as he stares up at me, his face not quite human. I love the idea that I'm bringing him to the edge of his own humanity. I've never had that power over any man, before Kyan.

Slowly, deliberately, I begin to roll my hips, driving my body up and down his cock, over and over, in a rhythm that starts slow and quickly becomes frantic.

He doesn't play nice, either. Instead, he meets me thrust for thrust, driving so hard into me that all I can do is hang on to his biceps and try not to buck right off him.

The dazed, heated look in his eyes is intoxicating.

I can only imagine what my own face must look like in this moment.

I can feel another orgasm building. My thighs tremble as his fingers find my clit; the light, teasing touch is all it takes. I wail and fall over the edge for a second time, and a moment later, he follows, jerking and pulsing deep inside me with a loud groan of release.

It feels like forever before I come back to reality. I'm sprawled across his chest—his not-quite-healed chest—and I roll off him with a quick apology. He pulls me in to his side, turning us so he can spoon me from behind.

I feel warm and sated, and for the first time in days, genuinely safe.

He nuzzles at my hair. "All right, little witch?"

I chuckle, and his arms tighten around me. "More than all right, shifter man."

"Good."

It has begun to rain outside. The steady drumbeat against the window of the bedroom and the shingle roof is soothing; the gentle noise, along with the rush of endorphins from our lovemaking, has my eyelids growing heavy.

It's so cozy in here. Like we're the only two people in the world. I wish we could stay here a while.

It is only a fleeting thought, but it brings comfort. Tonight, at least, I can pretend that it's true.

"Huh," Kyan says.

I'm halfway to sleep already, but—in stark contrast with the admittedly few other guys I've been with—he still seems pretty alert.

"What?" I murmur. With our bodies pressed together like this, I can feel the thud of his heart, steady and reassuring.

"Nothing. Just..." He presses a kiss to the top of my head. "A witch and a shifter. Who would've thought?"

"Indeed." I grin sleepily and wriggle my butt against him. His scent rises up, fresh like the forest outside, overlaid with the heady tang of sweat and sex.

"Go to sleep, Topaz." His whisper is close to my ear. "I'll keep watch, and wake you at five a.m. We can shower and be out of here before anyone is the wiser."

"But...don't you need to sleep, too?"

"I'm a shifter—I can go without for a couple of days. All good. Rest now." His voice is unexpectedly tender, and my heart flutters in response.

Then sleep overtakes me like a dark wave. If he says anything else, I don't hear it.

12

I WAKE SLOWLY, with a sense of bone-deep satisfaction weighing down my limbs.

Kyan is gone from the bed. My breath catches, then I see him in the armchair by the window, staring with a distant expression at the almost-dawn landscape. His trousers and boots are on, though his chest is bare—the blood-soaked and ripped shirt is probably in the bathroom, along with my blood-stained clothing.

His dark hair curls against his jawline, and his muscled arms rest loosely on the chair's armrests.

He's so gorgeous, even like this. *Especially* like this, in contemplation.

A gentle rain is still falling. In the gray early morning light, the droplets shimmer like silver. The pond—a small lake, really—is still and peaceful, a tranquil oasis that I'm sure was the reason these cabins were built at this location.

I know that my newfound safety—the serene haven we created for ourselves here—won't last much longer. But for now, I slide out of bed, wrapping the sheet around my nakedness and padding across the room to stand beside him.

"Morning."

His head turns and his eyes soften as he looks me over. "Hey. You're awake."

"So are you." I frown. "Did you really keep watch all night?"

He shrugs, resettling in the chair. "Of course. The danger is still out there somewhere."

"Thank you. Are you feeling okay? Must be uncomfortable in that chair."

Ky chuckles. "I told you, I'm a shifter. The chair is perfectly fine, and now that my wound is healed, I'm back to full strength."

"I'm glad. I'm feeling much better, too. My magic is probably even up to the task of fixing our ripped and bloody clothing before we head out of here."

"Shame." His smile crinkles the corners of his eyes. "I kind of like you wrapped in that sheet. Or even better... without it."

Heat rushes up my neck into my face and I duck my head to hide my embarrassment. I'm not used to this kind of intimacy; it feels awkward, the morning after.

A glint of something shiny catches my eye and I turn,

grateful for the distraction. Amethyst's silver box lies on the bedside table. My heart beats extra-fast as I pick it up and stroke the lid.

Meet me under the river.

My cousin is waiting for me. Today's the day we find her, and figure out what to do about the demon threat.

Kyan is watching me. I'm newly aware of the delicious ache in my limbs from last night, and the unfamiliar soreness between my legs. An image of the two of us rutting hard and fast rises in my mind, and I wish we had time for a re-do.

But we can't. It's time to dress and get out of here before the owner twigs that there's a pair of squatters in the cabin.

"Do you want the shower first?" I ask tentatively. "Or..."

"I took one an hour ago. You go ahead."

"Okay." I set down the box, still not quite meeting his gaze, and scurry to the bathroom.

When I'm done showering, I lay out Ky's shirt on the floor and cast a repair spell over it.

It is a simple incantation and with my magic levels restored, doesn't take long at all.

The ripped fabric knits nicely, and as I watch, the bloody stains disappear, until the shirt is as good as new. I do the same with my top, covered in Ky's blood, and then dress quickly.

As I'm about head out, I notice a small bowl on the dresser, filled with fragrant dried flowers. I scoop out the flowers and fill the bowl halfway with water before returning to the bedroom.

Ky eyes me as I hand him his repaired shirt before setting the bowl on the bedside table.

"What are you doing?" His tone is curious, not judgmental, and yet I can't help but feel self-conscious.

"Scrying," I mutter. "Or attempting to, at least. Jury's out on whether it'll actually work. It's not my strong suit, that's for sure."

I avert my eyes from the delectable rippling muscles as Kyan pulls on his shirt, and return my attention to the bowl, trailing a hand through the water's smooth surface and watching my own reflection break and reform.

"Scrying," Kyan says thoughtfully. When I look up, he runs a hand through his hair. If possible, it's even more rumpled than before. I try to hide my smile, and tamp down the hint of jealousy—if I did that all the time, my hair would look ridiculous. He just looks sexier, the messier it gets.

He gives up on trying to neaten his hair and wanders across to look over my shoulder. "What is scrying, exactly? Is it like looking into a crystal ball? Seeing glimpses of the future?"

"It's like divination," I say. "Gaining some insight into whatever it is a person needs to know. In this instance, I know roughly where Amethyst is hiding, but I'm going to scry to try and figure out *exactly* where she is."

"Good idea. We can then work out a game plan on the way."

His hands drop onto my shoulders, and I relax into his touch. I feel so comfortable with Ky, as if I have known him for far longer than a couple of days.

He gently squeezes my shoulders before stepping away.

"I'll go forage in the other room for something to eat."

I nod gratefully, glad of the space. It'll be easier to focus without the distraction of his presence.

Scrying works best if the seer has some kind of personal item belonging to the person being sought. The only things of Amethyst's I have on hand are the silver box, and the cleansing salve I put on Ky's chest. The latter will be easier to hold. There isn't much salve left, but I dig through my bag to find the tub and clutch it in one hand before closing my eyes and gathering together every memory of Amethyst I have.

The images fill my mind, growing more and more vivid with each passing second. Sunlight through a car window. A bare, freckled arm reaching up to the sky. Giggling on a beach, breathing the salt-smell of the ocean on a rare day trip. Sharing secrets under the cover of darkness, after the clock struck twelve.

Her face blooms in my mind. Sharp, high cheekbones. Wide brown eyes, just like mine. But where my hair falls in ordinary brown waves, hers is a deep, sleek chestnut.

Focus. Breathe.

I open my eyes and stare into the bowl of water.

Neon lights appear on the surface—hazy and indistinct at first. Then, the image sharpens. A restaurant sign appears above a bustling establishment: *The River Bar and Grill.*

I smile down at the bowl.

"Yeah, I got *that* part already. But where are you, Ammie? Where *exactly*?"

The scene shifts and wobbles. My vision travels down a narrow set of concrete steps to a basement area, through an almost hidden door in the corner and past a beaded curtain into a long hallway. I finally reach a small room, where a woman sits hunched over a desk.

My cousin.

She's surrounded by books and ingredients. Half-finished spells litter every surface of her workspace. The red brick wall above the desk is covered with neat lines of protection sigils. I watch as the warding flickers, sensing my presence.

Amethyst looks up, frowning.

My breath catches as her eyes skate past me. I want to tell her that we're safe, that we're coming. But I know she won't be able to hear me. After a moment, she returns to her work. My presence is nothing more to her than a whisper on the wind.

My fingertips breach the surface of the bowl, and the image dissolves.

I swallow my disappointment and stand up from the bed, wishing I'd boosted the water with a droplet of blood. I might have been able to communicate with her. But it doesn't matter. I have all the information I need.

Kyan chooses that moment to re-enter the bedroom. He is juggling two mugs of coffee and a bunch of granola bars.

"It's all they had left in the cupboard—though the coffee is hot and fresh. Nothing fancy, I'm afraid."

"We don't have time for fancy." I gesture to the bowl. "I know where my cousin is."

"One of these days I'll make you a real breakfast." He winks. "I have a killer French toast recipe."

"I'll hold you to that."

"I'm counting on it."

We sip on coffee and pick our way through the snacks until we've had our share, bickering over what constitutes acceptable breakfast food. It's strangely normal, and I can almost kid myself that this is our life; that Kyan is about to walk out the door on his way to work, kissing me goodbye as he goes, before I head off to my shop.

We don't talk about what happened last night.

Neither of us wants to break the spell. His eyes linger on me as I braid my hair, and I can't help but think about his hands in it, firm and certain as he guided my mouth to his cock.

But we can't pretend forever. It's time to leave.

I grab my bag and start to pull out a bunch of money for the cabin owner, but Kyan stays my hand.

"No."

"But—"

"No. The pack's got this." His expression brooks no argument. He leaves a wad of cash on the kitchenette counter, more than enough for the night's accommodation, and to cover cleaning costs and the food we ate.

After a brief hesitation, I nod. "All right. Thank you."

I cast one final wistful look behind me before the cabin door closes. For all I know, the few hours we spent here will be the last shreds of normality I'll ever have again.

I know what's coming for me. It's on the horizon already —a black, desolate cloud hanging over everything.

It was always going to be this way...

His hand, solid and warm on my arm, tugs me out of my daze.

"Hey," he murmurs. "You know I'm here, right? I'm not going anywhere."

Unexpectedly, affection bubbles up inside my chest. My hand comes up and covers his.

I don't trust myself to speak, but Kyan seems to get the message anyway. We fall into step beside one another as we make our way to the car.

"So, where next?"

"When we were growing up, my cousins and I bounced around a lot," I say. "One time, Ammie and I ran away from our foster parents—Sapphire was too little to come with us that time—and we ended up hanging around outside this bar down by the beach."

Kyan smirks. "Couple of little tearaways, weren't you?"

I shoot him a rueful smile and shake my head. "Couple of little idiots, more like. Lucky for us, the owners let us crash in their back room. They kept us safe till the social workers came. Could've got nasty, especially with our powers, which were really untrained and untapped, back then."

Kyan nods. Adolescence and magic do not go hand-in-hand. I'm sure he has more than a few stories of his own on the subject of teenage shifters.

"Anyway." As I lay a hand on the car, I stare off into the trees without really seeing them. "We used to say that if we ever got in trouble, we'd take baby Sapphire and head back down to that bar." I look across at him. "It's called *The River*."

"Meet me under the river," Kyan mutters, and then shakes his head.

As I pull out onto the track that leads to the main road, I take one last glimpse in my rear-view mirror. Everything peaceful and normal is now behind us.

Only the goddess knows what lies ahead.

13

Kyan

THE DRIVE IS UNEVENTFUL. At one point, Topaz turns on the radio and sings along to the oldies station. Her warm, low tones fill the car, but I can't share the moment; every mile we travel is a mile closer to her cousin.

Before we get there, I have to tell Topaz the truth.

"Topaz." I catch her attention and she stops singing. "We need to—"

"What if we're making a mistake?" The sudden question bursts out, distracting me from what I was about to say.

The radio drones on in the background. I reach out and turn down the dial.

"What do you mean?"

"It's…" She removes one hand from the steering wheel and casts about wildly, obviously trying to express whatever emotions are swirling inside of her. "I don't want to put Ammie in danger."

I frown. "She's already in danger." My tone is not unkind, but she flinches regardless. "You saw that mess back at the resort. They already know about her—which means, she'll be safer with us. Trust me."

I turn away from her to stare out the window. The undulating hills roll by. "Hellhounds prefer to hunt isolated prey. Far easier to catch and kill. There is safety in numbers—for you, and for your cousin."

Topaz shivers. "Hellhounds are monsters. Demon lackeys. At least Sapphire's far away from all this."

I don't reply. The radio fills the silence between us as we drive on. Each song begins to sound lonelier and more wistful than the next. I need to explain everything to her. Trust that the connection we've already formed will be enough that she doesn't run away.

I can't bring myself to say the words.

Hellhounds are monsters.

Coward.

It's nearing lunch time when we finally pull up beside the bar known as *The River*. A shiny row of motorcycles is parked out the front; they glisten in the sun, the light catching their chrome features.

"Nice." I circle the nearest one, studying it with narrowed eyes. "Nicer than mine."

Topaz blinks a few times. "You ride?"

I shoot her a look. "You sound surprised."

She shrugs, and a tiny smile plays about her lips. "You're just full of...layers. Just when I think I'm beginning to know you, another layer peels away to reveal something new."

Given the direction of my thoughts in the car, her observation is timely.

I open my mouth to blurt out my truth, but she has already jogged away from me and around the side of the building housing the bar.

I follow her and find myself in a dusty alleyway. It is shadowed and dark, full of dumpsters and bits of trash. I can hear the clatter of dishes and chatter from a nearby kitchen.

Topaz is already standing at a narrow doorway leading to a dark stairwell. She points. "Down there."

I nod, and sprint forward so I can take the lead. Who the hell knows what might be waiting for us down below? "Stay behind me, and if anyone attacks, I want you to take the car and leave."

Her eyes are wide and, after a short hesitation, she nods silently.

Satisfied, I tread down the stairs with my shifter stealth. Topaz is far noisier, even though she is trying to be quiet, too.

I figure I can shield her with my body if anyone is waiting below. Anyone other than her cousin, that is. Whoever—or whatever—waits for her at the bottom of these stairs, I'm glad I'm here to support her.

At the bottom is a sturdy door with an impressive-looking lock. I'm about to bend down and pick the lock when Topaz pushes past me and bangs her fist on the wood.

So much for being quiet.

"Amethyst?" She raps again. "Ammie, open up! It's me!"

There is silence, then...

"Topaz?"

The voice is muffled, tinged with fear and mistrust. Nevertheless, Topaz grins at the closed door like the Cheshire Cat.

"Yes! Oh, it's good to hear your voice."

There's a shuffling sound, and a couple of muffled thuds, like something heavy has been moved away from the entrance. The door opens a crack, and through the gap, a set of eyes studies us.

"Give me your hand." The woman inside hisses the command at Topaz.

"Oh, come *on*—"

"Hand! Now!"

She grits her teeth and extends her hand, glancing back at me and rolling her eyes.

"What the hell is she—" I start forward at the flash of a silver knife, but Topaz holds up her other hand.

She winces as the blade knicks her palm, extracting a drop of blood, before disappearing back inside the door. She cradles her hand at her chest.

"You okay?" When I grab at her hand to examine the injury, she sighs.

"She's just making sure I'm really... me. That I'm not wearing a glamor."

"And she had to maim you to do that?" I raise a skeptical eyebrow.

"It'll heal," she says, impatience in her tone.

Before we can get into it further, the door opens fully and a woman who looks similar to Topaz sweeps her into a tight hug. I inhale the smell of lilac-scented shampoo and herbs.

Like Topaz, and at the same time, not like her at all.

"Hurry, hurry!" She ushers us both past the threshold, barely sparing a glance at me before she shuts the door and draws a deadbolt across. She whirls around, wide-eyed. "Did anyone see you? Are you being followed?"

"No, not as far as we know, anyway," Topaz answers, her tone wry. "It's lovely to see you too, Ammie."

The room is small and low-ceilinged – some kind of converted cellar the bar above must use as a storeroom. Judging by the scattered ingredients and stacks of books lying over the desk, and a small fold-out sofa bed in the corner, it's obvious that Topaz's cousin has set up camp here.

"Oh, Ammie, what happened?" Topaz covers her mouth with a hand, and points to Amethyst. Twin scars trail down over her collarbone. The shape of the wound is hauntingly familiar.

Amethyst straightens up, frowning at Topaz.

"A hellhound." She traces her fingers over the scar absentmindedly. "I managed to injure it enough to get away, but it must be still out there somewhere. Hunting..."

She takes a long hard look at me.

When the color drains from her face, I know what's coming, but my voice closes over and I'm powerless to say anything to stop it.

Something flashes in the palm of her hand, and before I can move, she lunges.

I throw up my arms out of sheer instinct but her momentum is strong. We tumble backward into the wall. She lifts the knife blade to my throat.

My shifter rears up.

Amethyst is staring right into my face when it does, and she recoils slightly, but the knife remains where it is.

"What the *hell?*" Topaz pulls fruitlessly at her cousin's arm, but Amethyst shrugs her away with ease. "Stop it, Ammie! What are you doing?"

I stare at Amethyst, waiting for her to make a move. I could overpower her quickly, and I think she knows it, but she is obviously unwilling to back down.

Courage must run in the Redferne family.

I turn to Topaz. "I didn't want you to find out this way."

Her arms fold across her middle. "What do you mean?"

"I wanted to tell you... I tried a couple of times..."

"Be quiet," Amethyst growls, and my hand twitches up toward the blade. "Hey! Try it, and I'll bleed you dry."

If I don't diffuse the situation right now, anything could happen.

"He's been *helping* me!" Topaz is barely restraining herself; I can feel her energy crackle like static electricity in the air around us. "Yeah, he's a shifter—I *know* how it sounds—but I'm telling you—"

"*Helping* you?"

"You got something against shifters now?" She draws in a shuddering breath. "I thought you'd be more open-minded, Am. I thought you'd understand!"

"Topaz..." Amethyst's eyes flash with anger and fear. "This isn't *just* a shifter."

"Let *me* tell her. Please." I keep my tone gentle, but Amethyst's face twists.

"Fuck you!" Her mouth tightens. "My attacker shifted before he fled, and I got a good look at his face. His eyes. Those eyes haunt me every time I try to sleep. They were unmistakable. Unforgettable. Green. Until a bright shimmer of crimson madness takes over."

Topaz stares at me with the truth embedded in her gaze. She knows. Her cousin doesn't even have to say the rest, but she does it, anyway.

"Open your own eyes, Topaz. This creature is a monster. A hellhound."

14

Topaz

I JUST STAND THERE, unable to take in what Ammie has said.

Absurdly, I want to laugh.

I wait for my cousin to drop the knife, and explain that this is some elaborate, ill-timed practical joke.

No-one moves. Eventually, I take a deep breath and huff it out slowly.

"Kyan." I can't keep the slight tremble from my voice.

"She's wrong, isn't she? You're some kind of hybrid wolf shifter, right? You're not... you can't be..."

A hellhound. A hunter for your demon masters.

I can't even say the words out loud.

His gaze fixes on the wall behind me, his expression like stone.

I drag a hand over my face. The ground tilts beneath me, and I sink down onto a nearby crate, suddenly afraid that my legs are going to give out beneath me.

Details resurface in my mind. Things I overlooked, small and large, falling in rapid succession like a jigsaw puzzle piecing itself together.

The unusual appearance of Kyan's pack, so unlike any other shifters I've ever seen before. The strange, uncanny carvings in the room I stayed in on pack lands. The way he seems to know so much about hellhounds—how they would find us, and how precisely he predicted all our enemies' movements.

And the blood. The same color blood as the hellhounds at the resort.

How did I not realize?

A nasty voice in the back of my mind pipes up. *Maybe I did.*

Maybe I just didn't want to see Ky for who or what he really is. Maybe I was blinded by lust, to what's been here, right in front of me.

I close my eyes. Coldness spreads through my chest, slow and inexorable.

Hellhounds will do anything to get close to the ones they're hunting.

So, was it all a lie? Every touch, every glance. Every minute of passionate intensity. Every fleeting moment of companionship. The shaky trust that we've built up. Was all of it... meaningless?

I shared my bed—and dared to dream of something *more*—with a creature who would likely see me dragged, screaming, down into the pits of Hell.

I stand up. I'm not shaking any more, though the hurt of betrayal still courses through my veins. More than anything, I'm furious—only I'm not sure if it is directed at Kyan, Amethyst, or myself.

"I'm sorry." Amethyst's gaze is unyielding, but there's pity in her expression. "These creatures..."

She shrugs, but I ignore her, focusing on Kyan. "Tell me she's wrong," I say again. This time my voice comes out in a whisper. "Ky, tell *her*."

He makes no effort to escape Amethyst's knife still hovering at his throat. On the contrary, he doesn't seem to register her presence at all as he begins to speak.

"Topaz, I was not hunting you. *Or* her." He nods toward Amethyst. "Let me explain."

"What is there to explain?" Amethyst snarls. "If you've done anything to harm her, I swear to the goddess—"

"I would *never* harm Topaz," Kyan spits back, keeping his stormy gaze pinned on me. "Please. I wanted to tell you..."

"So, it's true?" I back away, ending up at the opposite wall. I splay my hands out against the brickwork, to stop myself from falling.

"What's true is that our pack does owe your mother and aunt. We owe *you*. And your cousins." He flicks a glance at Amethyst and then back to me. "Nothing that happened between us was a lie, Topaz. Nothing."

The green of his eyes is so intense I feel as if I'm drowning. I swallow hard as images assail my mind. Kyan holding me tight, pounding into my body, both of us writhing and moaning as waves of pleasure roll over us...

I hunch into myself. "Why keep that a secret?"

"I know you have no reason to trust me. Not now."

"Trust?" My fury finally decides its target is all Kyan. "You lied to me! I will *never* be able to trust you."

Real hurt flashes across his face before his expression smooths over. He grabs the knife out of Amethyst's hand and flings it to the floor so hard it pierces the wood and quivers, right next to his own foot.

Ammie sucks in a shocked breath and jumps back, but instead of making any move toward either of us, he slouches back against the wall. "I didn't lie. I omitted part of the truth. You need to hear me out."

"No, I don't. You need to leave."

His presence has me spiraling; self-hatred and panic churn in my gut. I can't believe I've bedded a hound of death —a hunter for the very demons I am trying to evade.

And I led him straight here, to one of only two people in this world I call family.

Amethyst moves to my side and takes my arm. Kyan glances between us before his jaw sets, and he turns toward the door and unbolts it.

In silhouette like this, he's a stranger to me again. With the broad lines of his shoulders, and his imposing height, there is no trace of warmth or friendliness in his stance.

"Lock the door behind me. Ward it. Do whatever you need to do, and stay safe. You and me. It wasn't a lie."

He takes one final look at me, his eyes full of unreadable emotion, and then he's gone.

Amethyst slams home the bolt.

"Here, drink this."

I look up blankly, as Amethyst presses a steaming mug into my hands. I take a sip, inhaling the fragrant scent of herbal tea. She collapses onto the low sofa bed beside me. Mercifully, she doesn't say anything else, just lets me sip at the hot liquid until the tight feeling in my chest eases somewhat.

When I finally set down the mug, she nods with approval. She slides her chunky silver bracelet up and down her wrist. It's a familiar, nervous gesture that usually bothers me.

Right now, the action is soothing. It reminds me that I'm not alone.

"You slept with him?"

I release a mirthless chuckle. "It was that obvious?"

"Err...yes."

I nod. "I didn't know he was a hellhound." I don't raise my head to look at her. I just let the words sit in the silence between us. Then I add, "Actually, I think part of me suspected he was." She deserves the truth.

"I don't blame you, hon."

"That makes one of us."

Her hand on my forearm makes me want to pull away, but when I try, she just grips tighter. "Come on. Hellhounds aren't exactly your average shifter. There was no way you could've known, for sure."

I swallow down the shame that threatens to bubble up to the surface.

"Yes, there was. I even tested his blood when he first turned up at my house. It displayed as a color that wasn't even listed in Mom's spell book. The same color that showed up when I tested that blood at your resort. I figured you'd put that there for me to follow the trail, and

I didn't question why it might be the same color as Kyan's."

"Ah. The blood. Yes, it came from a hellhound who had the misfortune to test the strength of my protective wards at the property. While it was incapacitated, I evacuated the place—luckily, we were closed given some renovations are due to start next week, so there were only a couple of other staff members there. Then I lay the trail for you, and high-tailed it out of there before the injured creature woke up."

"You could have just left a proper note."

She raises a brow. "Could I? Really?"

I think back to the pack of hellhounds. To Kyan's insistence they would never give up the hunt. To Ammie herself, and how her brain works in mysterious ways. "Yeah, okay. Maybe not."

Amethyst sighs. "The real question is, why are they here?"

"You know why. Ammie… we knew this day would come eventually. He's back." I drop my head, burying my face in my hands. "Luthor."

Even the name sends a shiver of dread down my spine.

My own personal grim reaper.

"Maybe. But I don't think it's as simple as Luthor coming for you, Tee. I think it's bigger than that."

"Do you think the Otherworld is rising?"

"Yes. I think it is." The fact that she doesn't disagree with me, raises the tension even higher. "I think there are cracks appearing in the fabric of reality. I've felt it coming for a while. Creatures who normally live in the shadows, are being set loose in our world."

Hellhounds. Demon wraiths. And that means… demons.

"Yes. I don't know what changed. I mean, the Winter Fae magic held things steady for a while, but now…"

"Could it be the Accord and what happened a few months back? There was all that unrest in the Winter Court."

"Maybe," I say. The Accord Agreement that all magical and supernatural species have signed—promising to live in peace and harmony here in the human world—almost fell apart during a coup attempt in the Winter Court of Faerie. Chaos reigned, until Rhodri, Maewen and the latter's half-banshee sisters helped to bring down the truly evil exiled Fae queen.

"Perhaps something happened when the Fae's attention shifted to that nutter, Queen Rhiannon."

"It's possible." I'm not exactly sure what has changed, but something has. Luthor has haunted my nightmares for so long. The fact that he is sending creatures after me now, means he's likely in a position to collect what he believes is rightfully his.

My soul.

"We'll figure it out." Amethyst is in full flow now, ever ready with a pep talk, even in the face of impossible odds. Hearing her tone—so certain and steady—I almost believe it myself. "Just like we did last time. Right?"

After a beat, I nod.

Her face floods with relief. Clearly, she had been expecting a fight. "So, we'll relocate. Get on a plane—"

"No."

She raises a brow. "What?"

I shake my head and get to my feet. All at once, the stress of the past couple of days—Kyan turning up, the wraith attack, the pack and their disclosure about our mothers, the hellhounds, and then Ky's betrayal on top of it all—comes flooding over me.

I've been buying time, running, but the clock has run

out. My magic can't sustain itself at these levels forever—and the stress alone is likely to kill me long before Luthor gets his chance.

"I've had enough, Ammie. I'm not running anymore."

She opens her mouth to protest, but I wave her down. "No. You know it as well as I do. We don't have the strength to hold them off forever. And we can't hide for long, no matter where we go. It's time to end this. To take a stand and face whatever comes."

And if Luthor ends up taking my soul, then maybe he'll leave Ammie and Sapphire alone.

Her eyes widen. "Are you sure?"

"One way or another, he'll find me," I say simply. "I'd rather it be on my terms, and on my turf, than his."

Maybe I'll go down. In all likelihood, I will. But I won't be dragged from my bed in the dead of night. I won't run endlessly from place to place. I won't spend another day looking over my shoulder, waiting for my fate to find me.

I won't be hunted any longer.

Something resolves itself in my cousin's expression, and she gives a slow nod. Once Amethyst has made a decision, she acts on it without hesitation. Before I can ask her what she's doing, she pulls out her phone and dials.

"Sapphire?"

My heart squeezes. *No!* I mouth, waving my hands frantically.

I haven't seen Sapphire face-to-face in almost a year. Her powers make her hypersensitive to people's emotions, and the hustle and bustle of the city drives her nuts. It's the one thing that I think has kept her off Luthor's radar, and I intend to keep it that way.

She's safe in the countryside.

I want to grab the phone out of Amethyst's grip and

throw it across the room, but she holds me at arm's length as she explains the situation to her sister in a low, calm voice.

When she finally hangs up, she glowers at me, her hands on her hips. "She's not a child anymore."

"I know that! It's just... It's *me* Luthor is after. I've dragged you into this mess, but I don't want to do the same for Sapphire, if I can avoid it." In my mind's eye, I can picture her, pale-skinned and dark-eyed like us, with long, chocolate-brown tresses. She has none of Amethyst's flinty resolve or quick temper; none of my endless self-doubt. She is quite probably the most powerful witch of the three of us, but part of me still can't think of her without remembering the innocent little baby she once was.

"We need her," Amethyst says, following my train of thought with her usual uncanny accuracy. "And there's safety in numbers, right? She's potentially exposed, out there on her own."

Safety in numbers. Kyan said the exact same thing.

I'm forced to concede the point. If anything happens to Sapphire while she's alone, I won't be able to live with the guilt.

I shudder, trying, for the millionth time, to figure out how it has all come to this.

Everyone I love is in danger, and it's all my fault.

I look up at the sound of a metallic clink. Amethyst is hunched over her desk, examining a spell in the open book in front of her. She's fiddling with her bracelet again. She looks pale but determined.

A similar sense of purpose floods through me. I'm not going to drown in self-pity, not while I have people to protect.

First things first.

"We can't stay here." I gesture at the bare brick walls. A

thudding bass sound, muffled, filters down from somewhere above us. Outside, footsteps and distant voices indicate that the bar above is growing more crowded as the day gets later. "We're in the middle of the city. Too many people around if..." *If it all goes to shit.*

"I agree." Amethyst moves her thumb over her phone screen. She holds up the phone. When I see the location on the GPS map, my heart sinks.

"We're meeting Sapphire there?"

The taste of salt in the air. A stormy sky overhead. The scream of gulls over crashing waves. Fear. Death.

"You know it makes sense," Amethyst says. "It's the one place where we all—"

"Yeah." I cut her off before she can get any further. "Okay. Fine. My car's outside."

"No. We can take mine instead. If we leave now, we can make it before dark."

Amethyst begins rolling a bundle of dry herbs into a piece of cloth and securing it with a neat bow. "Help me with this lot."

"What?" I glance around the room. It looks as if someone has raided an apothecary in here. "All of it?"

"Use a little magic. Won't take us long. Soon enough, it'll be the three of us against the world, once again."

I know Ammie is merely being flippant to try and lighten the mood, but I can't help thinking that this time, it really is, us three against the world.

The Otherworld.

15

AMETHYST DRIVES us out of the city.

I can't keep my thoughts from drifting to Kyan.

Was I unfair, not letting him explain?

Surely, he proved himself on my side, in the time we had together?

I wish I'd been less shocked and more open to listening, given our shared experience. I mean, he nearly died trying to protect me.

Guilt spears through me, and my thoughts tumble endlessly, without a solid conclusion.

It is a relief that Ammie has the wheel right now.

We spend the first half hour or so in silence, then I manage to rein in my wooly thoughts, and share what I have in mind.

The plan is simple, really. Especially now that Sapphire will be involved as well. Our magic will be stronger than ever, with the three of us there.

Basically, we are going to turn on its head everything that we have been doing up until now. Instead, we are going to do the reverse.

That means no more hiding behind protective wards; living our lives with one eye staring over our shoulders. It means tearing down defenses, and bolstering our magical signatures until we practically become one giant beacon. Anyone hunting for us will be able to locate us from miles away.

Then, we will use my blood to create a summoning spell.

Truth be told, I'm pleased for the distraction, even though I am terrified of what might be about to happen. Any lapse in our conversation brings my thoughts straight back to Kyan. I can't think about him without wanting to break down and cry.

Stupid. I've only known the guy five minutes. Why is he taking up so much mental real estate?

It is late afternoon by the time we pull up at the beach. As soon as I alight from the car, the years melt away. The area is exactly as I remember—miles of white sand under a wide sky, heavy today with rolling banks of clouds. The dry grass along the verge of the path rustles against my calves as the two of us trudge down between the dunes and onto the sand.

A shiver runs down my spine. I shut down memories

that are too difficult to deal with and concentrate on putting one foot in front of the other.

Beside me, Amethyst touches my elbow. "She's waiting for us."

Our eyes meet, but she hurries ahead before I can reply. I don't have to ask how Amethyst knows. She and Sapphire have always been aware of each other's whereabouts. Their bond used to fill me with jealousy, but now I'm simply glad for them, that they have such a strong sister connection.

As we exit the dunes, I catch sight of a slender figure standing at the shoreline. My heart rate picks up.

Sapphire has her back to us as we grow nearer. Her arms are wrapped around her thin frame, a scant form of protection against the elements. The wind is fierce out here, and her hair whips around her pale neck.

She doesn't turn, but says anyway, "Ammie and Tee. Hey gals."

"You know, Sapph." I raise my voice so she can hear over the rush of wind. "Most people use their *eyes* to see with."

She does turn, then. A smile lights up her face and she rushes toward us, giddy with excitement.

"Oh my!" I stumble backward as Sapphire hugs me tightly. "So good to see you, kid!"

"Long time, no see," she murmurs, before bobbing away. She wrinkles her nose in a gesture so familiar that I laugh out loud. "And enough with the 'kid' nonsense. I'm twenty-five."

"Sorry. Force of habit."

Last time we were on this beach, Sapphire *had* been a child—a tiny toddler in overalls, clambering over the rocks. I swallow and push the image away before it pulls me under.

She greets Amethyst in a similar manner, enduring a million questions from her older sister ranging from, *are you eating enough*, all the way to, *I hope you're getting out of the house, you're looking kind of pale,* until I take pity on her and cut Amethyst off.

There's little time for niceties after that.

We choose a spot halfway up the beach to perform the ritual. Luckily for us, the gray and windy weather means the stretch of sand is deserted.

This is definitely not the kind of thing for an audience.

We all know exactly what to do.

It has been years since the three of us came together like this. It doesn't matter. Time and distance fall away as Ammie, Sapphire, and I work together with easy, practised motions. Like clockwork.

We have our differences, in personality and in magical ability, but right now, it doesn't matter. We are witches by blood, and the same blood runs through our veins. Elements of the same *magic trace* run through our veins.

The sky rumbles overhead as if in portent, as my cousins begin to draw concentric circles in the sand around us. Using Amethyst's blade, I deepen the cut she made earlier on my hand and sprinkle the resultant blood into the grooves of the circles. As I do so, I whisper an incantation.

Instead of seeping away, the blood spreads, creeping out to fill the shallow wells and form dark rivulets all round us. I watch as each section joins together. Dark patterns begin to form, arcane symbols of summoning that I have mostly only seen laid out in books.

Goosebumps rise along my forearms as I start to second-guess myself.

What are we doing? This is ridiculous.

My cousins should go into hiding, and I should just go back to the Fae and ask for their help once again. Even if giving and taking favors from the complex and often-devious Fae can sometimes be even more problematic than the issue at hand.

"Don't," Sapphire says, as if sensing my self-doubt. "This is the right thing to do. I know it, Tee."

I shoot her a sheepish grin and continue my spellwork.

Amethyst dumps an armful of candles onto the ground. One of them rolls toward me, and I stop it with my foot, bending to pick it up.

"Where did you get these from?"

"I always carry them." Amethyst shifts from one foot to the other, looking defensive. "Just in case. You're not the only one with a big handbag full of tricks."

I exchange a glance with Sapphire, who merely shrugs, a smile playing at the corners of her mouth.

I place the candle where Ammie directs me to, and then watch as she places the rest of them. She digs each one into the sand so they can all stand upright on their own.

Sapphire, always good with fire and light, waves an arm around in a twirling circle, and the candles light up all at once, like the little beacons they are.

Then both of my cousins look at me, and I nod once. "All right. Let's do this."

We link hands and begin the summoning spell.

At first, I don't see anything. Then shadows begin to form outside the circle. The patches of darkness lengthen and stretch. The sand shifts, and the darkness solidifies around us.

Hellhounds.

A whole pack of them, prowling outside the widest circle. Amethyst and Sapphire stand with blank, pale faces on either side of me. I'm sure my face is equally pale. I squeeze their hands, and each of my cousins squeezes back, before we all let go.

We are in this, together. Whatever happens, now.

I can hear the low, rumbling growls of the hounds over the sound of the ocean waves. The memory of their hot breath and cavernous sharp-toothed maws from the resort attack turns my stomach.

I try not to think about Kyan. About the tenderness in his green eyes when he looks at me; the gentle touch of his fingers on my body...

No. Shut down those thoughts.

Behind the hellhounds, more shadows form, and then demon wraiths appear.

They look human—mostly. Their eyes are hollow. I can't tell what they're cloaked in; at first, they appear to be in ragged clothes, but then I realize the air around them is shifting like a mirage. It is the darkness itself that is clinging to them.

Clothed in darkness.

The very definition of evil.

The wraiths don't speak. They don't need to. Terror rips through me and it is all I can do not to drop to the ground and curl up in a whimpering ball.

A slight sound issues from my throat, and I swallow hard, determined to show no weakness. Not to these creatures. The minions sent by Luthor.

To distract myself from the horror of what is in front of us, I raise my chin and pretend a bravado that is all illusion.

"Where is Luthor? He sends all of you, but doesn't come himself. Is he afraid to show his face?"

The wraith nearest to the circle hisses something unintelligible. The hellhound pack presses closer.

At a glance, I count at least seven or eight hounds and four or five wraiths. It is hard to pinpoint the exact number, when the shadows keep shifting. For all I know, there could be a hundred more hunter hounds or wraiths lying in wait, just on the other side of the rift between this world and their own.

It doesn't matter either way; we're hopelessly outmatched.

I turn my head and meet Amethyst's wide, frightened gaze. She knows it too; there are too many of them.

My voice trembles as I speak again. "Where is Luthor?"

The monsters around me don't respond. It is as if I haven't spoken at all.

My heart thuds so hard it threatens to leap out of my chest. I can't hear much beyond the roar of the sea, and the rush of blood in my ears, and that growling sound from the surrounding pack—a sound that is becoming louder by the second.

If Luthor doesn't appear—if my cousins die on this beach, trying to protect me...

"I demand an audience with your master!" I shout the words as loudly as I can. My magic, entwined with my cousins', crackles through the air around us. Sand drifts down from the shallow dunes behind us, and the seagrass rustles, whispering in a sudden gust of wind. "Luthor. I'm here. I'm not running any more. Come on, show yourself!"

One of the hellhounds snaps at the air near the circle. Sapphire is nearest and she flinches backward, even though the creature does not attempt to cross the ward.

Not yet, anyway.

A snickering sound, like beetles scuttling over a wooden floor, fills the air.

The demon wraiths are laughing at us.

Hopelessness rushes through me.

What were we thinking, that the three of us could go up against a demon soul collector, and come out on top?

All the 'should-haves' and 'could-haves' rush into my mind. I should have gone to the supernatural police and Inspector Maewen Jones for protection. I should have run, like Amethyst suggested.

I could have called on the Fae Winter Court to help me —they did once before, and I know they would, again. Even if the Fae always demand a favor in return, it would have been better than *this*.

Most of all, my heart aches because I sent Kyan away so heartlessly. Now, I will never know what it could have been like to have a relationship with someone who made me feel so special.

I've doomed myself—and my cousins—to certain death on this beach today.

My eyes catch a flicker of movement on the sandy ridge above us.

I look up and a gasp rushes out of me.

Eyes. Deep, dark red. A whole row of them glowing in the unnatural twilight.

More hellhounds. Dozens of them, all fixated on the action about to unfold down here.

Watching. Waiting.

My heart catches in my throat. There's something familiar about the one in the center of the pack. The wide shoulders; the long legs. The sharp tilt of its head; the way its ears prick up as its gaze slides over mine and holds for a single, burning moment.

A shiver runs over my skin.

Kyan.

His pack stand with him, shoulder to shoulder, hackles raised and lips curled up in silent snarling readiness.

How could I ever have mistaken them for wolf shifters? They are nothing like any other shifter I've ever seen. These creatures are enormous, with their long legs and their huge shoulders and intense yet deadly expressions. Even the smallest of them would tower over me, should I ever dare to stand beside one in this form.

These shifters clearly belong to the Otherworld. They look out of place on this windswept beach, silhouetted against the pale sky, even with the demon wraith shadows surrounding us.

The whole pack must be here with him. My heart leaps. At first, I wonder if it is fear that drives the adrenalin spike, but then I realize... it isn't fear. Its *elation*.

I don't know how I know, but I do—Kyan is not here to serve any demon master.

He and his pack are here to protect the bloodline of the witches who helped them. My mother, and my aunt.

The Redfernes.

Ky's heart has proven to be true. He is here to save me. If he can.

There's a low growl from directly beside me. My head snaps toward the sound. The demon wraiths are close, hovering just outside the circle. And their hellhound hunters look as if they are readying to leap, regardless of any protective ward that might harm them.

The wraiths aren't laughing any more.

Slowly, the one at the center of their shadowy group raises its hand and then drops it through the air.

The hellhounds lunge. The shadows engulf us.

And that's when all hell breaks loose.

Literally.

16

Kyan

No! She's mine.

I howl a warning at the rival hound trying to take off Topaz's head. Our pack explodes into movement.

We are eager for the hunt.

We spring from the ridge like a seamless, well-oiled machine, our numbers easily overwhelming those of the demon wraiths' hellhounds.

I lock eyes with Topaz. Her posture is rigid; her mouth

wide with concentration as she knocks back the hound beside her with a flurry of magic. In this form, I cannot offer her comfort. I cannot offer her anything, but my hellhound body and my fighting spirit.

I hope that will be enough.

I take a mighty leap into the fray below, landing directly on the back of a wraith, knocking it to the ground and tearing at its neck, before the creature disintegrates beneath my jaw and my unsheathed claws.

I raise my head, seeking her out.

There she is, among the smoke and falling ash.

She is magnificent in her black dress, with her hair flowing out around her and with crimson magic spooling from her palms—she looks like a goddess born of blood and fire.

My mate.

Mine!

She stands back-to-back with her cousins. All are facing outward, confronting the demon horde and flinging their magic barbs everywhere.

Hope flares in her expression as she briefly meets my gaze.

Warmth blooms in my chest. I wear the hellhound form, and yet, she hasn't flinched away in horror or disgust.

Does she recognize her mate, regardless of my physical exterior?

She squares her shoulders and nods in my direction, and then she's gone, lost again amidst the shadows and fighting bodies.

The certainty that I will do anything to protect this woman—*anything*—has nothing to do with the Redferne name, or with any pack promise.

I will not lose Topaz, when I have only just found her.

The witches' circle has already been breached. I race forward, needing to get to her side, needing to protect her from all the horrors of the Otherworld.

Horrors that I know intimately.

Horrors that I grew up with.

Horrors exactly like me.

A demon wraith ahead of me raises a hand, and with a single, withered finger, points straight at Topaz's chest. Right at the spot where her heart lies.

No!

With a roar, I launch into the air, arcing toward the monster that would kill her. An enemy hound catches one of my back paws in its jaw and yanks me down.

I kick out and roll, writhing to gain traction, and then the creature is on me.

Then another. And then a third.

I snap and bite, swiping viciously with my claws and teeth, bloodlust taking over until all I am is a killing machine.

Finally, there are three black-furred bodies lying in a heap. A gap in the smoky darkness appears ahead of me and I barge through, aiming for my mate.

How is it possible that she's still standing, shooting out magic all over the place? She is so strong—far stronger than I ever realized.

Her cousins are no longer with her, but I hear the yells and snarls and screeches around me and I know they must be dishing out their own magic punishment just as fiercely as my Topaz.

As I lunge across the sand, she raises a hand and directs a jet of fire directly into a demon wraith's cold, dead eyes.

The creature swats the fire away and the magic fizzles out, leaving a long scorch mark over the beach.

"Little girl," it hisses, lips peeling back to reveal blackened, pointed teeth. The voice is a sibilant whisper, and yet its message reverberates loudly through the air. "I was forged in the flames. They burn hotter than you can ever imagine, let alone conjure from your measly store of magic. Your party tricks cannot harm me."

"Maybe not, but I *can* slow you down."

Her voice is barely there, but I am so tuned in to Topaz that I can hear her even several feet away. There is fear in her tone, but also determination. My heart surges with pride at my mate's courage.

Even in the face of death, Topaz refuses to give up.

I reach her side at the same time as Burley. I share a glance with my Alpha, but there's no time for anything other than positioning ourselves between her and the demon. Thick, dark smoky fog unfurls around the creature, crawling toward where we stand.

I bare my teeth and growl at the creeping menace.

Before I can launch at it, a spell whooshes past my shoulder and hits the ground right at the demon's feet. A deep crevice appears in the sand, and a sinkhole forms around its feet, dragging it down into the earth.

"How's that for a party trick!" Topaz screams toward the space where the demon is sinking.

Unlike the fire, this spell seems to weaken the demon. The fog retreats, and Burley manages to get close enough to snap at one of the wraith's bony hands.

The creature moves so fast, there is no time to send a warning to Burley. One moment, my Alpha is snapping his jaws and growling, the next, he is impaled on the demon's clawed arm. It reaches right into Burley's chest and punches through to the other side of his ribs, coming out halfway along the hellhound's back, with Burley's heart clutched triumphantly in its claws.

My own heart stops for a moment as the connection between Burley and every member of our pack is instantly severed. Completely and irrevocably.

A whine escapes my throat, and then I lower my head and charge at the monster. Only I'm too late. Far too late. The fabric of its robe melts into the wind, vanishing completely, as does the demon itself, leaving only the collapsed body of my Alpha on the bloodied sand.

Minus his heart.

Pack voices rise in my mind. *Our leader is dead. You are our Alpha now, Kyan.*

I do not wish to take that role.

But now, I have no choice.

I raise my muzzle to the sky and howl my grief, my heart breaking as I say farewell to the man who was the closest thing I've ever known to a real parent.

Topaz

The sound of a grief-stricken hellhound pack is something I never want to experience again.

Their collective howling wail tears at my eardrums, until I hunch into myself, covering my ears to try to ward off the unspeakable sadness and despair.

My eyes well, misery called forth by the hellhound lament, until my cheeks are covered in tears. I think back to the gruff yet welcoming man who led the pack Ky belongs to. I hardly knew him, and yet, his absence will be keenly felt.

I can't even imagine what it must be like for Ky and his fellow pack members. Does it feel as if part of him has died in this moment? I want to run to the howling monster in front of me and wrap my arms around him. Give him comfort amid his grief.

I'm so sorry, Kyan. For everything.

And yet, I don't have time to process any further thoughts on the tragedy. The demon wraith I was fighting, and most of the enemy hellhounds, might be gone, but Amethyst and Sapphire are still locked in battles of their own on separate parts of the beach.

Ammie has somehow ended up atop the ridge, facing a gigantic shifter beast with teeth that look like long knives. My pulse stutters when it turns its head briefly, and I catch a glimpse of its blind, empty eye sockets.

Is that one of the hounds I blinded earlier today in the forest?

Its lack of vision ability doesn't slow it down: if anything, it fights more fiercely than it did at the resort, lashing at Ammie and one of Ky's pack hellhounds with its claws, and snapping its jaw with an enormous cracking sound every time one of them gets too near.

Down here on the beach, Sapphire faces a demon wraith. Her long hair whips around her in the unnatural wind, and for the first time I see how much she's grown up. The small girl I once knew—and the gawky teenager who followed— are both gone. Unaccountably, she bursts into wild laughter, her eyes bright. Silver magic radiates from her body.

She is beauty and power intermingled.

And she is having *fun*.

From behind me comes a deep, rattling breath, like dry leaves rustling in a graveyard.

Shit. Stop worrying about everyone else.

I still have my own battle to deal with.

And Luthor hasn't yet appeared.

Kyan growls beside me as I turn and face a demon wraith in the process of dragging itself up from a rift in the earth. I dare to lay a hand on Ky's shoulder, hoping that is okay with him in this form. He leans into me, as if lending me his strength.

Relief rushes through me and I take a second to simply enjoy the heat from his furred body.

Thank the goddess. He doesn't hate me, even after I sent him away.

I picture what we must look like in this moment. A hellhound and a witch, working together.

Falling for one another.

The absurdity would make me laugh, were the situation not so desperate.

Even in his grief for his Alpha, Ky's focus remains on helping me. I clench my fingers in his soft fur, hoping he knows how much I appreciate his support, and then remove my hand and allow my power to surge inside me. This time, I enchant the rustling grasses around us. Under my magic, the blades lengthen and spread out, forming thick ropes that snake around the wraith's arms and torso.

The monster is stuck, half in and half out of the ground. It twists and thrashes as its robes begin to singe and smolder, burning away as the magic ropes them.

An ear-splitting whine from the ridge above confirms that Ammie has just sent the last hellhound packing.

I don't turn. I can't take my attention off what I'm doing. Ammie jumps down into the sand beside me and adds the strength of her magic to my own.

My muscles tremble with the sustained effort of holding off the creature.

The grasses grow faster, binding the demon into place through sheer force of our combined wills.

"Remind me to get some pointers from you when all this is over," Amethyst huffs, panting with the effort. "You've been practising your nature magic."

"What can I say? It keeps things fun at parties." I grin, though I expect it looks more like a grimace. Together, we bury the demon under a mountain of grass and sand, pushing it down, down, deeper and deeper, until I can no longer feel its energy imprint at all.

"We need to help Sapphire!" I squint, trying to make her out in the storm of magic, smoke, and dust around that area of the beach. "Where is—"

A scream comes out of the whirling storm, and a burst of adrenalin surges in my system. I gape as Sapphire flies through the air and hits the rocks beneath the ridge. I make out her slumped form, her ashen-white face. Blood.

I charge forward, my mind blank with fury. I can't hear anything but the ringing in my ears.

The demon turns its head. Its mouth twists as its eyes lock onto mine, and it sends out a rolling cloud of something dark and creeping with a single flick of its clawed hand. The dark ribbon starts from under its cloak and races toward me over the sand. In its wake, the grassy plant-life withers, blackening and dying before my eyes.

At the last second, I throw up a shield, my arms trembling with exhaustion.

I already know that it won't be enough. I'm almost completely drained of magic.

The only emotion I have left to channel is despair.

We lost. And Luthor didn't even turn up.

My spell is too weak; it flickers like a guttering candle. The black mist eats through the remnants of my magic like it is made of tissue paper.

I have nothing left. The realization is almost peaceful.

I can stop fighting now.

Once they take my soul, maybe my cousins—and the rest of Kyan's pack—will finally be safe.

I bow my head and wait for the darkness to engulf me.

It never arrives. Instead, just as my shield fails, Kyan leaps in front of me, taking the full brunt of the magical attack. Another hellhound grabs the wraith in its giant maw and rips the monster's head right off its shoulders.

But it's too late. I barely have time to scream out, *"Kyan!"* before he collapses in the sand at my feet.

17

I'M VAGUELY aware of movement all around me. Everything is muted, as if I'm underwater.

I drop to my knees and sink my hands into Kyan's thick pelt. I can't sense any sign of life.

No pulse, no lifting of his ribs to denote breathing. Nothing.

Finally, I raise my head to find Ammie and Sapphire standing over me. There's blood and sand in Sapph's tangled hair. She's trembling, but her gaze is lucid, and her grip is firm when her hand lands on my shoulder.

"Is he dead?" she asks. I flinch at the emptiness of her tone. She must be as drained as me.

And Ky...

I release a sob. "I don't know. I think..."

I can't say it out loud. I don't want it to be true.

Around us, the battle seems to have died down. The remaining demon wraiths and enemy hellhounds have vanished. All that is left are small groups of Ky's shifters, clustered together around their injured, and their dead.

A shadow falls over me, and I swipe a hand across my face, drying my tears, before looking up.

A hellhound looms over us. He is almost as big as Ky. The fuzz around his muzzle is flecked with a touch of gray, and he has a jagged scar—an obviously old injury, not from today's battle—showing through the fur on his right flank.

I don't know who this is, but he is staring at Kyan as if willing him to live.

I get to my feet and the shifter transfers his stare to me. It feels like a battle of wills. I will *not* drop my gaze. Eventually, the hound bows his head slightly as if in supplication, and then lopes off.

What was that about? I don't speak shifter language.

A tiny noise, so faint that I almost miss it, catches my attention.

The hound lying at my feet is gone. In its place, a naked Kyan lies curled on his side... and now I can ascertain the faintest movement of his chest, rising and falling.

"He's alive!"

I crouch, my heart rate thundering as I scan him from head to toe. There is no visible sign of injury; his skin is unbroken. Why is he not awake? Something is wrong.

He shifted back. Is that a good sign?

"Ky?" I whisper.

He doesn't respond.

"Okay." My voice is full of false cheer, but I can't seem to stop. "It's okay. You're totally fine. I've got you—and I'm going to heal you again, all right?"

I press a hand to his breastbone and gently roll him onto his back. He's like a dead weight. I shove down the panic threatening to rise, and feel for his heartbeat. It is faint and thready, but it's there.

"This'll be three for three. You'll owe me big time after this one, shifter man."

My voice trembles, but Ky shudders slightly in response. Is that...a laugh?

"What did you go and do that for?" I ask. He's so cold, like he's taken a dip in icy water. After getting used to his higher-than-average body temperature, the coolness is frightening. "I had it under control."

"Didn't...." His eyelids flutter. His hand creeps out and touches my wrist, but then he releases a whimper. Even that small movement seems too much for him.

I bend down, close to his ear. "Don't talk." I stroke a stray lock of hair away from his eyes. "I know that's hard for you, but just try, okay?"

A faint smile ghosts about his lips.

Please don't let this be our last conversation. I don't want the last words we say to each other to be laced with sarcasm.

Still, the sound of my voice seems to calm him. He remains still as I lay my hands on his chest again, more firmly this time.

I look up at my cousins. They watch us both with carefully neutral expressions.

"Will you help me? You know healing isn't my strongest suit. And, I don't have much left in the tank."

Without hesitation, both Ammie and Sapphire step forward and kneel down beside me.

"Of course," Sapphire says. "I don't have much left, either, but what I have is yours."

"Me too," Ammie adds. "We need to wake him up properly, so I can apologize. What do you need from us?"

"He's seems to be freezing. We need to counter it with warmth. Restore the balance."

I use magic to cut my finger and swipe blood across my other palm. I have so little power left; I need the direct touch of my blood to boost the spell. Then I concentrate, allowing the warming spell to flood through me. I feel my cousins' magic entwine with mine—the dreamy quality of Amethyst's and the fierce, almost battle-like dark-light from Sapphire.

Slowly, heat leaches from my palms and into Ky. Starting where my hands connect with him, directly over his heart, I visualize healing energy spreading to every region of his body. His skin begins to return to its natural tawny hue as the blood magic flows.

When I look up, I realize we have an audience. The whole pack is gathered around us, their gazes fixed on Kyan.

He shifts beneath my touch, moaning and half-opening his eyes before he settles.

When his body is properly warm, I withdraw my hands and allow myself to exhale.

I sit back on my heels in the sand, and wait for him to wake fully. And then, I wait some more.

Kyan—sexy, stubborn, impossible Kyan—seems to have fallen straight back into unconsciousness.

The next few hours pass in scattered fragments.

I move in a dreamlike state, only half-listening to Amethyst as she leads us to a disused beach house a little way up the shoreline. I let her drag me up the front steps to the porch, my hand trailing over the peeling white paint on the handrail.

Behind us, the pack is mostly silent. A couple have retained their shifter forms, but the majority are human again. The fact that there are a whole bunch of naked people hanging around us on the beach, feels like the least weird thing that has happened the past few days.

Some of the pack took Burley's broken body and disappeared somewhere—whether back to the pack lands, or through some portal to their Otherworld origins, is unclear.

Others from the pack are injured; Sapphire weaves her way through the group as they straggle over the sand behind us. Her face is pale and strained. She must be close to the end of her energy. And yet still, she reaches out to push a burst of healing energy through the wounded every so often.

Sweet Sapphire. *Strong* Sapphire. How does she still have anything left in the tank?

Not for the first time, I consider that Ammie's little sister might be the most powerful witch of us all.

That is a thought for later. For now, I need to focus on Kyan. He is still unconscious. One of his pack mates carries him, flanked by two other men. All the shifters' faces are like stone, but I know it's a façade. Their leader fell in that battle, and it isn't guaranteed that Ky will make it, either.

The pack are likely just as terrified as I am.

They carry Kyan up the steps of the cottage, and one of the men shoulders open the front door after Ammie pushes a small burst of magic into the lock. Inside, the house is neat and homely. Judging by the leaflets pinned to the notice-board in the kitchen, it's some kind of holiday cottage. Lucky for us, there's no sign of occupation at the moment.

I exchange a silent look with Amethyst. She merely shrugs in a very un-Amethyst-like manner.

I guess we're breaking and entering.

It seems to be turning into a habit, for me.

I can't bring myself to care. I follow the shifter carrying Ky up to the next level, to a small bedroom overlooking the sea. He lays Ky out on the bed and turns to look at me.

"We were never introduced. I'm Dane. Kyan's second, now that Burley is..."

Raw pain flares in his expression.

"Dane. I'm so sorry for your loss."

He nods and, noting the flecks of gray in the man's dark hair and the jagged scar on his right hip, I realize this was the hellhound who nodded at me earlier. I stare at him, unsure what it all means. Was he acknowledging me earlier? As Kyan's healer, or his *mate*?

"Um, when you say you're Ky's second, does that mean—"

"It means Kyan is our new Alpha."

"I...see."

And I do. The desperation in the air is almost palpable, and now it makes more sense. The pack have lost their leader. They cannot afford to lose another, within the space of an hour or two.

"Do you know what's wrong with him?" Dane's question is straight to the point.

My heart squeezes in my chest as I move closer and lay a hand on the coverlet beside Ky's arm.

"I don't know." My voice is thin, almost a whisper. I hate that I feel so powerless. "The demon wraith sent something after me. I've never seen it before... It looked like a ribbon of black but there was no scent. It wasn't smoke, I'm sure of it. I couldn't stop it. It just kept coming. And then Kyan leapt in front of me and... the black ribbon seemed to disappear right inside of him."

I trail off as Dane's eyes flare red, as if he doesn't like what I've said. And yet he remains silent for a long moment, before turning to stare out the window.

I follow his gaze. Outside, the sea is calm and bright. No trace of the death and destruction that graced the beach a short time ago. On any other day, the view would be a peaceful one.

"Kyan is like a brother to me," Dane says, his voice gruff. "I would die for him, if I had to."

"I believe you."

He grunts. "It took him a long time to settle into his role in our pack." Dane turns his gaze back to me, and his eyes are shadowed. "He kept acting out, refusing to acknowledge his place with us. Not wanting to accept that he might one day need to step up as Alpha. And then, one day, he began to accept. Now that the day is here..."

He might not live long enough to take up the mantle.

He doesn't need to say the words out loud. I can almost hear them in my own head.

I think back to the other night. Kyan's firm body pressing me down into the mattress, the feel of him inside me. The complete *rightness* of our coupling, despite the horrific circumstances of our meeting.

"I won't let him die. But I need to know about the black smoke ribbon thing. I saw it in your face. You know what it is. Please tell me."

Dane pins me with a dark stare. "That black smoke... demons call it Shadow's Bane. One touch of the stuff will stop the heart of most mortal creatures—supernatural and non-supe alike."

Shadow's Bane? Fear clenches tight in my chest. "But... Kyan isn't dead."

Dane's mouth twists. "Like I said, *most* mortal creatures. Kyan comes from the Otherworld, from the place where demons rise. To him—to *us*—their magic isn't quite as deadly."

I cast a glance down at Ky, like his eyes might suddenly snap open. "Then why doesn't he wake up?"

"If it was Shadow's Bane that felled him, then he still took a direct hit of demonic energy." Dane lays a hand on my arm before he crosses the room. In the doorway, he lingers. "Hellhound shifters are tough, but that kind of magic... there are no guarantees.

"We are hot-blooded creatures, Topaz. Born from the pits of Hell. Shadow's Bane is designed to freeze the life out of anything it touches. Keep him warm, and pray to whatever deities you believe in. He'll either wake up, or he won't. We'll stand guard to keep you safe in the meantime."

18

BORN from the pits of Hell.

He'll either wake up, or he won't.

Dane's words run through my head on a continuous loop.

How can a creature from the Otherworld—from the very depths of the pit itself—be so caring and brave and strong as Ky has proven to be? How can I have fallen for such a creature?

Shifters and witches—*hellhounds* and witches, even more so—are sworn enemies.

How has it come to this? I am lying here on a stranger's bed, cradling in my arms the man I can't bear to lose, plying him with the warmth of my body and my healing magic and praying that he will survive.

He's a hellhound!

And yet, somehow, I've managed to fall for him.

I watch Ky's chest rise and fall under the white sheet that covers him, and snuggle my cheek against his shoulder.

An idea is forming in my mind. A stupid, crazy idea, for sure. But I'm sick of waiting around, powerless, for the soul collector to find me. Threatening those I care about. Putting everyone in peril. Losing people along the way.

Burley. I send up a silent prayer. *Thank you for your support of my family. I am sorry I brought you and your pack to this.*

I stroke Ky's jawline. *Don't let these bedsheets become his shroud.*

A soft knock at the door startles me out of my reverie. I sit up, wiping a couple of stray tears that have slid, unbidden, down my face.

"Come in."

The door creaks open. Amethyst's face appears.

"Topaz." The door opens wider, and she steps into the room. Her brow furrows and she crosses her arms. "Have you slept? Or eaten?"

"Yes," I lie. "A little, earlier."

Her face softens. "You know there's nothing more we can do, right? Come downstairs for something to eat, and then come back and get some rest."

Reluctantly, I slide out from under the covers and rise to my feet. Ky doesn't stir as I move away. In the doorway, I turn back one last time.

Nothing.

If it wasn't for that slow, shallow breathing, and those couple of brief awakenings earlier, I would assume he was dead.

I follow my cousin along the narrow hall and down the stairs. Before we reach the main living area, however, I grab her by the arm. Muffled voices drift through the closed door. I'll get everyone up to speed eventually, but right now, I need to talk to my cousin. Alone.

She follows me into the small kitchen pantry, frowning when I close the door behind us. It's a little too cozy; I barely have room to flick on the light switch, but it'll have to do.

"What?" Her eyes dart over my face. "You look like you have something unpleasant to share."

I release a wry chuckle, though the sound contains no humor. "You could say that."

I can't keep this to myself any longer. Still, now that the moment has arrived, I'm frozen. I just stand there, my gaze fixed on cans of kidney beans and lentils on the shelf behind Amethyst's head.

"Well?" she demands.

"I never told you the full story of why Luthor's coming for me." I say it in a rush.

Amethyst stills. Something flickers behind her eyes, as if she's processing the information.

I swallow. "Remember when I told you the Winter Court Fae solved my...err...my problem?"

Her eyes narrow. "Yes?"

"Well." My voice gets shakier. With every word I speak, the reality of what happened grows. "I told you some of what happened. You know Luthor is after me. But I didn't tell you everything."

"Uh huh. Okay, then. Spill."

I swallow hard. "The problem was... I died."

"What?"

"Not... not *fully*." I flinch at the expression of anguish that floods her face. I want to take back the words, shove them deep inside, but I push on. "I was *supposed* to die, I guess you could say."

Amethyst shakes her head, dazed. "Oh, my God."

"Yeah. As you know, the Winter Fae brought me back. Healed me." I pause. "But... they used old magic to do it. I've never seen anything like it, Ammie. Not before or since. They saved me. And the act went against the natural order of things."

"What do you mean, *supposed* to die?"

"It was a long time ago, when I was first experimenting with my blood magic. I didn't know what I was doing, and I ended up not being able to stop the stream of magic. It burnt a hole in my chest. Leached everything from me—my blood, my energy, my very life..."

I shudder at the horrific memory. "Somehow, I accidently called forth a soul collector from the depths of Hell."

"Fuck!"

My mouth drops open for a second. I don't believe I've ever heard my cousin swear before today, and this make twice. I swallow down my shock and continue. If I don't admit it all now, I never will.

"If the Winter Fae hadn't interceded, my soul would've passed on to the Otherworld, courtesy of Luthor."

I stare down at my feet, unable to meet Amethyst's gaze. Afraid of the censure and blame I might read there. "King Rhodri—well, he was merely the Winter Court's heir apparent, back then—happened to be in the area with his mother. She simply stood there and watched, with a smile on her face... but Rhodri ordered his warriors to carry me back to Faerie."

"Why did you never tell me this part of the story?"

I do look at her now, but there's no blame. Only shock, and fear.

Because telling someone would have made it real.

"Because I was afraid." My voice is a whisper. "All that weird stuff was already happening in the Winter Court. I'm not sure why or how, but I think maybe Rhodri's mother, Queen Rhiannon, might have had something to do with it."

Ammie's gaze narrows. "If that *bitch* had anything to do with what's happening with us now, then we're all fucked."

"*Ammie!*"

"Well..." She shrugs, defiant. The thing is, she's likely correct. The former Winter Queen caused destruction and death for many years, from her stronghold outside Faerie. It was only a few months ago that my friend—and shop customer—Inspector Maewen Jones, managed to kill her with the help of her banshee sisters.

"Maybe she did. Who knows? Rhiannon certainly loved chaos and destruction. Imbalance and imperfection. Everything that I tapped into that day. When I was there, in Faerie, there were whispers that they shouldn't have used the old magic to help me... that they should have let me die. That the power transfer knocked something loose in the ether—something that isn't covered by the Accord."

Amethyst tips her head. "But the Accord Agreement covers all supernatural beings and magical creatures. *All* of us..."

I smile grimly. "Except the celestials. Angels and demons. Remember?" The skin on the back of my neck prickles. "Portals are opening up everywhere, Ammie. Maybe it's not just about me anymore. Maybe I started it, through my foolishness. But if the Otherworld is rising..."

"Then we're all in danger," Amethyst whispers. "For real. Jesus, Topaz."

"I'm sorry." Misery threatens to pull me right under. "This is all on me."

Amethyst drags me into a hug so tight that all the air squashes out of my lungs. "No. It isn't. Maybe it started with a little spell experimentation by you, but we never had anyone to show us how to do it properly. I'm older than you—"

"By what? A couple of months?"

"Still. I'm the oldest. I should have helped you learn how to deal. Blood magic is more difficult to master, Tee, than dream walking, or scrying, or anything else Sapph and I can do. But I didn't help you. I left you to figure it out alone. So, it's as much on my shoulders as it is yours."

"That's beyond ridiculous. That's worth another swear word. Fuck's sake, Ammie. I mean... *fuck's sake*."

She gives me a little shake. "We can swear all we like, but the problem is much bigger than either of us, now. We'll fix this. No matter what it takes, we'll work it out."

"How?" My time in the Winter Court was brief. For obvious reasons, I've tried hard not to think about it in the months and years that followed. Now, I force the unwanted memories up to the surface of my mind, trying to piece together the fragments of recollection. "What's the first rule of magic?"

"Um..." She shakes her head, confused by my seeming change of topic. "Balance? Every piece of magic has a counterpoint. Energy given, and energy taken away. Like a set of scales."

"Exactly." The air in this tiny space feels too close, too hot. "My 'death' is an unresolved event, stopped by magic that should never have been wielded."

"So, the soul collector—"

"Luthor." I close my eyes. "He came for me, and stood on the side lines as the Fae kept him from taking my soul away."

The memory is hazy. The burning wound in my chest. Choking, unable to breathe. Floating above my broken husk of a body as I lay on the floor of an enormous chamber. Golden light surrounded me. The Fae gathered around, staring down at my body and then up at me. I realized they still saw me—the *real* me; my essence. I remember they stood silent and watchful, forming a barrier around my unresponsive physical form while two of them worked their strange magic.

"I didn't belong in their realm... but neither did *he*. He couldn't cross the threshold, not fully. It bought them enough time to reconnect my soul to my body, and then they sent me back here to the human world."

"So, maybe the key lies in Faerie?"

I smile at the hope in her voice. "Not exactly. I do have something in mind, Ammie. A plan, of sorts, but you're not going to like it."

She grips my arms. "Yes, we have a plan. We go to the Winter Court and ask the Fae for help to return things to how they were."

"It's not that simple and you know it. The soul collectors are no different from any other creature in that regard. They might be hideous demon monsters who revel in death and pain and destruction. But they crave *balance* as much as anyone else." I gesture down at myself. I am exhausted and dirty; my clothes are rumpled and sand is stuck in my hair. "To them, I'm a walking contradiction. I should be dead, and I'm not. They're not going to *stop*, Ammie. Not until they get what they want."

Amethyst's throat works. "A soul for a soul."

"Exactly." I stay silent for a long moment. "I die, or someone from my blood line does. Either way, they're determined to take what is due. And if we anger them too much, then they won't care. They'll try to take us all."

I push open the door of the tiny pantry and step back out into the hall. "But I am equally determined not to let that happen."

19

IN THE END, I put my plan on hold for a short while, and trudge back to the bedroom to stay with Ky. I conjure myself some buttery toast with jam and, after I've eaten, curl up again around the shifter's still-cool body and snuggle in, boosting my heating spell and relaxing only when I feel the warmth seeping back into his limbs.

I must drift off at last, because dawn appears to be breaking outside when next I open my eyes. I hear muffled voices in the corridor outside the small bedroom. As I wrestle out of sleep, the sound of arguing grows louder.

I lie in bed for a second, listening, trying to orientate myself, and then turn and stretch lazily...

And realize that I'm alone in the bed.

I sit bolt upright, the bedcovers falling away from my torso.

My heart thunders in my chest, until I recognize the arguing voices beyond the door.

Amethyst.

And Kyan.

"I told you, she needs rest! We couldn't pry her away from you—"

"Get out of my way, witch."

Ky's growl sounds as if he's only just hanging onto his temper. Scrambling out of bed, I stagger over to the door. Opening it, I find Amethyst blocking the doorway. And just behind her...

"You woke up!" I say, somewhat stupidly in the circumstances.

His mouth curves up, and the simmering anger in his eyes softens into something else. Something equally strong and powerful.

"So did you." His voice washes over me, familiar and enticing. A lick of desire heats my veins and I hang onto the door handle to steady my suddenly shaky legs.

Amethyst looks from one to the other of us, and then rolls her eyes, begrudgingly stepping aside and muttering something.

Kyan doesn't pay her any attention at all. He looks almost fully recovered. A little pale, perhaps, but otherwise much better. His eyes are bright as he looks me over. I know that he's checking for injuries, but I'm flooded with self-consciousness, nonetheless. I'm acutely aware of my flimsy borrowed nightgown and the rising flush in my cheeks.

For a moment, we just stand there.

The silence is broken by Amethyst, who lets out a groan. "I'd tell you guys to get a room, but..." She gestures behind me. "Wow, look at that. Already done. I'll leave you to it, shall I?"

She disappears down the corridor without a backward glance.

I get the strong sense that I'll be on the receiving end of an Amethyst-style lecture later, but right now, I can't bring myself to care.

"I...err..." Kyan shifts from one foot to the other. He rubs a hand across the back of his neck. "Sorry for disturbing you, Topaz."

His formal tone—such a marked departure from all our other interactions—freaks me out. But I let it go. After all, the last time he was in human form and fully conscious, I told him to get the hell out of my life.

Something has changed since then. Something deep and irrevocable. We are both in brand-new territory. There are no secrets between us, not anymore.

"It's okay," I say, stepping back so he can enter the room. As he does, the stiff line of his shoulders relaxes. "Amethyst can be a little..."

Ky raises an eyebrow. "Overprotective? A pain in the butt?"

"Dramatic." I sit on the edge of the bed. "She *was* apologetic about...um...the knife incident."

He snorts. "Yeah. She did apologize, earlier. She's still overbearing."

I agree, but I don't think it's the time to admit that out loud. Instead, I focus on the view outside. Through the half-drawn curtains, the tide is coming in along the beach. The sky is clear and cloudless; it is going to be a beautiful day.

"We're family." I try to explain it to him. "Ammie and Sapphire are my coven sisters as well as my cousins. We have no one else, so we have to look out for each other."

"That's not exactly true," Kyan says, his tone soft. "Not anymore."

He sinks down onto the bed beside me, heedless of the rumpled covers. I feel another absurd prickle of self-consciousness; seeing his hand spread out like that, the smooth tanned skin contrasting against the white sheets, conjures up memories I've been trying not to think about.

"Kyan..."

"Topaz." He leans forward, forcing me to look him in the eye. "I'm so sorry. For all of it."

I blink back a wave of tears. I have a thousand questions, but I don't know where to begin. Eventually, what comes out of my mouth is barely more than a whisper. "That first night. Did you come to kill me?"

"No. To *track* you." He lifts his hand and runs it through his already-disheveled hair, staring past me toward the window. "Our kind... most of us, anyway... You've got to understand. We're not quite like other shifters."

I nod. I've figured that much out on my own.

"For other packs, there's a hierarchy that starts and ends with the Alpha. There is no higher authority. But for hellhounds, it's different. Of course, we have an Alpha—Burley was ours..."

"And now it's you?"

He nods. "But it doesn't end with the Alpha, for hellhounds. Most of us are in thrall to the Otherworld. If one of the higher-ups gives us a job to do, we do it." Kyan takes a deep breath. "The night Luthor came to us, his instructions were clear. Find the witch named Topaz Redferne. So... we did."

I thought back to the night the demon wraith arrived at my house. Finding Kyan, injured, in the middle of my back lawn. "Why didn't you just kill me immediately?"

Ky's mouth tilts upward at the corners. "For one thing, your wards kind of took me out of commission."

I duck my head, unsure whether to laugh, or scream and blast him with magic. Neither seems appropriate to the situation, somehow.

He huffs out a breath. "I *never* wanted to kill you, Topaz." A shadow falls across his expression. "You're a Redferne. That part of the story is true—your mother and aunt did help our pack, once, and we *do* owe them—and you, for their act of kindness. When it became clear the demon Luthor and his minions didn't share our concern, we took matters into our own hands."

"You went rogue," I guess out loud. My suspicions are proven correct when Ky slowly nods. "You *and* your pack."

"It was easy to convince the others. Burley wasn't sold on our marching orders from the get-go," he says. "Especially when he realized who you were. When the demons were ready to kill a Redferne witch? Not going to happen. Shifters do not break their promises. Not even hellhounds."

"I'm beginning to realize that." I tuck my feet beneath me and lean back on the pillows. We lapse into silence.

It has been no more than the better part of a day, but the time I spent watching over Kyan's bedside seemed infinite. In my head, I'd already come up with a thousand ways for this conversation to go. The Kyan of my imagination was understanding, horrified, sympathetic, and judgmental. Every shade of emotion under the sun.

The real deal sits opposite me, staring out at the ocean with one hand propped under his chin. His calm acceptance is far better than anything I could dream up on my own.

Now that the moment is here, the words stick in my throat. But I swallow down the nerves; after all, he has shared his secrets.

Time to share some of my own.

"There's a reason we're in this predicament."

Kyan narrows his eyes. "What?"

"On this beach," I whisper. "In this place. My cousins and I have been here before."

"Okay... I'm not following."

"Magic use leaves a trace, right?"

He nods. Basic stuff.

"Think of it like footprints left behind. Or scars." I twist my hands together. "Most of the time, it's small stuff. Everyday magic. The marks hardly show up, and most people don't notice the trace, unless they're really looking. But with bigger stuff—major spells—the place becomes important."

Kyan listens closely. "How so?"

"Well, whoever cast the spell can bolster their magic by returning to that same spot." I prop my hands under my chin, mirroring his position. "Think of it like... boosting the signal. And it's even more effective when there's more than one spell caster."

He raises an eyebrow, clearly taking time to digest this information. "Hold on. That bar where we found Amethyst..."

I chuckle. Trust Kyan not to miss a trick. "Yeah, exactly. Amethyst could draw off the marks we left there in our misspent youth to strengthen her spellcasting and protect her hideout."

He clicks his tongue against his teeth. "Damn. This is almost vampire-like."

At my quizzical expression, he adds, "The long game."

"Ah."

I can tell he's still pretty rankled by what went down at the bar. He and Amethyst aren't each other's biggest fans, if the altercation I overheard outside the bedroom is anything to go by.

"So," Kyan prompts. "What is it about this beach that's so special?"

I take a deep breath and let my eyes close. Memories rush to the surface. *Wet sand sinking under my sandals. The gentle breeze stirring my hair around my face. Amethyst's hand, locked tight with my own as we crouch beside the rocks, watching our mothers, tall and slender, silhouetted against the dark, crashing waves.*

I gasp and open my eyes. My face is wet. Kyan is at my side. He runs his broad thumb over my cheeks, drying the tears. I let him wipe them away, trembling, before I continue.

"We came here once before," I mumble. "When we were kids. Our mothers were working on a spell, you see. A new kind of experimental magic. They thought it might be possible to seal the rift to the Otherworld once and for all."

My eyes flick up as I remember too late where Kyan originates from. He doesn't interject. He just waits, patiently, until I continue.

"It was brilliant, really. They wanted to harness the power of the elements—create some kind of energy field." I sweep a hand through my hair. "But they couldn't get any other witch or mage on board. Everyone told them they were crazy to even try. So, they came all the way out here to run some experiments. They didn't want anyone to get hurt. But... they miscalculated something, I'm not sure what. All I remember is..."

I shudder, unable to finish.

A thunderclap that almost split the earth in two, followed by a flash of white-hot lightning, bright enough to temporarily blind me.

Amethyst—her piercing screams and her vice-like grip around my upper arm—trying to drag me back to safety, to where baby Sapphire lay sleeping in the car, parked up on the ridge.

Me begging Ammie to let me go, let me closer, where the power was surging and roaring.

Mom, I tried to yell, but I couldn't hear myself think. I couldn't hear anything but the storm.

Amethyst wanted us to be safe, out of harm's way.

I wasn't yet in double digits, but I knew there was no such thing as safe. Not for us.

Kyan watches me carefully while I gather the courage to continue.

"They didn't make it." I play with the edge of the bed cover, finding and worrying at a loose thread. "They couldn't control the power. The next thing I knew, I was back in the car with Amethyst and Sapphire. Mom and my aunt must have used the last of their magic to transport us away."

It's the first time I've ever spoken about what happened on the beach all those years ago. Even Amethyst and I have never talked about it. Part of me thought she must have blocked it out altogether—locked the trauma of our past in a corner of her mind—until she led us here, to conduct magic of our own.

"Magical signatures are hereditary," I whisper. "There are scars here. The memory of our mothers' magic... This place is full of it. We needed to bolster our power as much as possible."

"So, I guess they helped you out." Ky's voice is low,

matching my own soft tone. "Your mom and your aunt. They're helping you, even now."

I can't help but smile at the reassuring thought. This place has held nothing but bad memories for so long. Maybe now, there's some kind of silver lining.

"It still wasn't enough," I say. "Even with the boost from their traces, and the help of your pack, we barely held them off, Kyan."

The room is bathed in warm, morning light, but I still shiver at the horror of last night.

Kyan says nothing, which is confirmation enough.

A new thought occurs to me, and my breath hitches. "So... what now? What about Luthor? Are you still under his power?"

"No. He doesn't control us. The magic binding us to him disappeared for good the night we refused to help kill you. Something happened then—I think it might have been a leftover element of your mother and aunt's magic, perhaps, but since we broke free of any Otherworld influence, we are no longer in thrall." His intense eyes darken. "We can't return to the Otherworld, though. If we came anywhere close..."

He shakes his head, hair falling over his face. "I guess you humans might call us outlaws."

He shoots me a wicked grin.

Good, I want to say. Outlaws or not, I don't want the shifter pack going anywhere. I don't want *Kyan* going anywhere.

He must read some of this in my expression as his gaze sharpens. "Why? Were you worried about my wellbeing?"

"No!" I clutch my arms tight around my torso, before relenting. "Fine. Maybe a little. Happy?"

He laughs openly, his smile as bright as the sunlight that

falls over his face. I marvel at how naturally he carries himself in the human world. It's impossible to picture him as a creature of darkness. Even now that I have seen him in his hellhound form.

His expression flickers. He looks at me with a new intensity that makes my skin tingle. I reach up and cover my hot cheeks. I meet his eyes, defiant.

"Why are you looking at me like that?"

"You're beautiful." he says. Simple, like he's stating the color of the sky.

No one has ever complimented me like that before. So straightforward, and clearly not expecting anything in return. A gift that warms me to my core.

"Oh." *Smooth.* I don't know what it is about Kyan. He has a habit of disarming me with the smallest, most innocuous things.

Slowly, I lean in toward him. He wraps his arms around my waist, and I sigh at the feeling of rightness.

Last time we were alone in a bedroom like this, our coupling was frantic and messy. The undercurrent of urgency—the sense that we were running out of time—perhaps made us more reckless than we would normally be.

Now, we take our time, lying on the bed beside each other, face to face. He traces a pattern around my jawline, down my neck, and then follows his caress with his lips. He reaches my collarbone and then keeps journeying down, pressing kisses as he goes.

I wriggle to assist him as he lifts the borrowed nightgown and exposes my pussy.

He stops then, looking back up my body, and I arch toward him, trying to encourage him without words to continue his exploration.

Finally, he complies, trailing his tongue over one hipbone and across toward my mound.

I groan and buck upwards, trying to meet him part way. Trying to connect my most intimate place with his eager and talented mouth. He grins and turns slightly, almost but not quite touching me.

"Touch me, you goddamn shifter man."

He places his hands on my hips, steadying me, before he uses his thumbs to pull apart my flesh. He begins to blow on my clit and my head rocks back into the pillow.

I moan, unable to hold in my need any longer. I want him to give me everything and more, to make me forget everything that has happened in the past, and everything that lies ahead.

Eventually he takes pity on me. His mouth and tongue connect fully with my mound and he laps at my seam, circling and flicking my clit before exploring further. Going deeper. Finding and invading my channel with his hot and ready tongue.

I clutch at his head, my only reality in a sea of pleasure, and buck madly beneath his ministrations. The sensations rise, drowning me, until I can't take anymore. "I need you, Ky. Inside me. Please."

He moves away, removing his clothing, but the sensations he has created with his mouth are so strong I almost tip into orgasm just watching him reveal his stunning body.

His cock stands to attention, dark and ready, and I drop my thighs wide, waiting for him to join with me. The bedsheets twist in my hands as I pull at them, and I bite down hard on my bottom lip as he kneels between my legs and readies himself to enter me.

"I've never wanted anyone as much as I want you, little witch."

His words—those simple words—tip me over the edge into oblivion. I am already beginning to climax just as he thrusts into me, deep and strong, and I shriek as the pleasure of release rushes through every part of my body.

I don't care that there are others in the house. I don't care who might hear me. All I care about is my body clenching and pulsating around Ky's, as he pumps into me so hard my head almost hits the headboard at every thrust.

With a growling roar and an out-of-control bucking motion, he comes too, and the rush of heat as he releases his seed inside me creates yet another delicious meltdown.

I have never felt anything like this—so earth-shattering and all-consuming.

By the time we come back to earth, I'm a trembling, satisfied wreck. He folds me into his arms and I snuggle in, certain that I never want to leave this bed again.

20

THE SKY outside is dark when I finally decide to take action.

Beside me, Ky is still asleep. When I shift slightly, he mumbles something indecipherable, and his broad hand tightens around my waist.

I don't want to disturb him. How long has it been since he's had a chance to sleep naturally like this? A couple of days, at least. Not to mention, he's still recovering, especially after the day's... activities.

There's no point putting off this situation any longer. I can't keep running, and I can't keep hiding behind the ones

I love, hoping for a miracle. I need to take my fate into my own hands.

Carefully, I untangle myself from Ky and the bedsheets, and hop out of bed. I allow myself a moment to absorb the scene. The broad, bare line of his shoulders rises and falls gently as he slumbers on.

The house is silent as I creep along the landing and down the stairs, toward the back door. I use a muffling charm to keep the door from creaking as I open it.

The sand is cold between my bare toes as I pad down the beach. I spare one final glance at the cottage. Its pale, wooden façade is lit by moonlight, and no movement comes from the dark windows.

I turn away. If I stay here any longer, I'll lose my nerve.

It has to be this way.

The small metal bowl in my hands seems to grow heavier with each step. I clutch it to my chest as I hurry along, until the cottage is no longer in view.

I reach into my pocket and pull out the knife.

It's a small thing with a sharp, pointed blade. The handle is made up of precious stones, set in an intricate pattern. It glimmers in the moonlight as I hold it up.

The same knife, long ago, almost ended my life.

To an outsider, it might seem strange that I kept it. But it has been with me the whole time, hidden in a secret pocket of my shoulder bag.

I have no idea if this will work, but at this point I'm out of any other options.

"Luthor." I speak his name into the darkness. "I know that you're near."

I press the blade into my skin of my forearm, hissing with the sudden pain. A few drops of blood splatter into the bowl. I press harder, watching as a small pool forms.

"I feel your presence," I continue. "It's just the two of us, now. I'm not hiding anymore. There's nothing to fear."

"My child." I jump and my heart skips a beat. The voice comes from somewhere behind me. "What have *I* to fear from *you?*"

I turn, and there he is.

My demon nemesis. Luthor.

He doesn't look angry. Merely... curious.

I straighten my shoulders, refusing to show any trace of the terror that pulses beneath my skin, even though he will surely already sense it. "Your hellhounds might have a different view."

He doesn't rise to the bait. Instead, he smiles, inclining his head. "Shifter mutts. Yes, I hear you scorched out their eyes. Not bad for a witch."

He's mocking me. I watch him carefully as he walks slowly, arms behind his back, to the water's edge. If I didn't know better, I might take him for a genial uncle or family friend.

"Rumor has it you took another into your bed."

Cold rushes through me.

He turns then, regarding me with satisfaction. I hastily school my features back into something resembling nonchalance.

"I have to acknowledge, Ms. Redferne." He approaches me, unhurried. I want to back away, but I can't. It is as if I am frozen to the spot. "I'm impressed. It's not every day that a hellhound falls for a human. You are... quite remarkable."

He leans close. So close that I can't escape those black eyes as they pierce through me, looking deep inside. Searching for my soul. I feel as if icy water is trickling down my spine, and I begin to shiver.

"More remarkable still... you summoned me. You,

alone." Luthor uncurls one arm, lifting his hand up between us. His skin is stark white, and his fingers are tipped with black, pointed fingernails. He looks like an animated corpse. "Tell me. Why have you called me here, tonight?"

"To negotiate."

A cruel smile appears on his face. He tilts his head.

"I do not negotiate. And even if I did... what could you possibly have to negotiate with?"

"I have the one thing you're after," I point out. "My soul."

"Yes." For the first time, I catch a flicker of rage in his expression. It is gone in an instant, but it gives me hope. *He is not made of stone.* "It already belongs to me. I do not appreciate this charade. Give it to me, or I will take it from you. And if you make me take it... I will take them *all.*"

Just as I thought. He will never stop with my soul.

"I just want to ask you one thing." I pace a little way down the beach. *Don't let him see your fear.* "Why have you not taken it already?"

Luthor rears back, and the genial façade drops away. His true visage is so terrifying I have to drop my gaze to the ground. I close my eyes, waiting for his demonic retribution, but nothing happens.

Slowly, I open my eyes again. Whatever gripped him a moment ago, he is back in control. And he hasn't answered my question. "Death comes to us all in the end, child. Nobody can escape it."

"Pity."

Luthor eyes me. "Indeed."

"Tell me," I say. My voice is light, rhetorical: a mocking imitation of his own. "Can *you* escape it?"

His eyes widen as he notices the light beginning to emanate from my hands.

There's a burning deep in my core, molten-hot. Every

particle in my body heats up as my blood charges with the elemental magic I've been practising. The sky above rumbles, and my magic flashes against the darkness, illuminating the billowing banks of cloud.

I thought there was a storm coming, but I was wrong.

I am the storm.

Somewhere from beyond the wall of light, I hear Luthor's scream of rage. It is everywhere, permeating within and outside my mind. I want to drop to the ground and let the sand bury me. I'm drowning in power, just like my mother and aunt.

And just like them, it is growing beyond my control. I am merely a tether: a feeble conduit for the storm within me. I grow weaker with every second.

Soon enough, I will break.

And I know that at that point, he will have me.

"You think you can destroy *me*?" Luthor's voice floods through my mind, incandescent with fury. "You? You are *nothing*. Just like your mother."

I grit my teeth and hold on.

Maybe I can't destroy you, but I'm not nothing. Neither was she.

Luthor's physical form is failing. Deep cracks appear in the ground on which he's standing. The cracks spread and widen; they crawl up his body, splintering his limbs—and through the fractures, white light appears.

A low, rumbling snarl echoes through the blackness.

Even while I'm drowning in the magic that threatens to consume me, my heart leaps with fear for Kyan.

No! I want to scream. *It's too dangerous!*

The pack crowd in around me, a thick wall of fur and muscle, glowing red eyes fixed on their target.

And right at the center of them all, is Kyan.

He has never looked like this before. He is half-human, half-beast. He faces down Luthor with unrelenting fury. His eyes burn with just as much crimson intensity as his fellow shifters. The edge of a snarl tugs at his lips, and his knuckles flex, taut and white.

"Topaz Redferne is protected." His voice is guttural and not-quite-human, but even over the howl of the storm and the magic raging within, I can make out every word. "Tell every demon, every shifter. Tell every creature in the Otherworld."

The rage has suspended him somewhere between shifter and man. He pads forward on his bare feet, panting raggedly as he struggles to form the words. I have never seen anything more feral, or more beautiful.

I can barely take my eyes off him.

I tremble, struggling to hold on. Luthor is still weakening; it is now a battle of wills to see which of us will break first.

"This changes nothing." Luthor ignores the hounds who surge forward to rend and tear at his body. He only has eyes for me. "I will find you, witch! You are an *abomination*. You cannot be allowed to survive! Your soul is *mine!*"

The hounds still their attack, and then fall back, one by one.

Where Luthor once stood, there is nothing. Not a scrap of fabric, not a drop of blood. Nothing to suggest he was ever there at all.

Whatever is holding me up—whether adrenalin, fear, or a combination of both—abruptly deserts me. I fall to my hands and knees. I clutch at the sand, sucking in breaths, trying to calm my system.

Did I kill him?

I want to believe it. But I know that isn't possible. You

can't kill a demon; you can only force it back to the pit from whence it crawled.

I learned something tonight, at least. I learned that he cannot just step in and take my soul. It must be more complicated than that, and there must be circumstances that are needed, for Luthor to deliver me back into death. What those circumstances are, I have no idea.

But it is more information than I had a couple of hours ago.

The hellhounds remain a short distance from me. They sit, silent and watchful as statues. Waiting.

Eventually I find the strength to look up. The dark sky above is graying, shot through with streaks of blue-gold. Dawn glimmers on the horizon, gilding the sea and lightening the landscape.

A cold breeze brushes against my face. I tremble, letting out a heaving sob.

Warm arms encircle me from behind.

Kyan.

All trace of the shifter is gone. It's just the man now, familiar and comforting. Boneless with exhaustion, I let him pull me back against his firm chest.

"Hey," Kyan murmurs as he strokes my hair in a rhythmic, soothing pattern. "It's okay. I've got you. You're okay."

Eventually, my exhausted sobs subside. I sit up and look around for the pack, but they're nowhere to be seen.

Together, Kyan and I sit in silence, and watch the sun rise over the restless sea.

21

WHEN WE MAKE it back to the house, we're greeted by a fretful Sapphire and an Amethyst about ready to explode with rage.

"What the *hell* were you thinking, Topaz?" She rushes at me from the open door, pulling me into a tight, furious hug. "Want to explain what you were thinking, running off like that on your own? What happened to sticking together?"

"I'm sorry." The apology is muffled against her shoulder.

I want to explain my reasoning: how I figured out that Luthor would show himself to me, and me alone. Somehow,

I get the sense that it's not what my cousin needs to hear right now. I slide my arms around her and mumble more apologies, and she squeezes me tighter in wordless acknowledgement. There will be time for explanations later.

When Amethyst pulls back, her gaze lands on Kyan. He's hovering behind me.

"So." She puts her hands on her hips and gives him the once over.

"Ammie…" I trail off, too exhausted to deal with her temper.

"It's okay, Tee. I'm woman enough to admit when I'm wrong." Amethyst's mouth twists.

I glance at Ky. He tilts up his chin, waiting.

"You really do have Topaz's back. I see that." She gives him a short, sharp nod. "I was wrong. And… thank you."

"My pleasure." His serious expression fades away. A smile creeps across his face. "Does this mean we're friends, now?"

Sapphire, watching from the porch, laughs.

"I wouldn't push it if I were you," she calls out.

Amethyst's eyes narrow. "What she said."

She jerks her chin toward Sapph, and then suddenly we are all laughing together. Most of it is probably slight hysteria, but the sound helps my tight muscles to release a notch.

"Can we go inside, please?" I ask.

Ky lifts me into his arms. "Of course."

He carries me in to the lounge area and places me carefully down on the sofa. He sits beside me, holding my hand in his.

Now that we're back here, I don't know what to say. I grasp around for the easy intimacy of yesterday or last night, trying to recall the steady comfort of Ky's arms after Luthor vanished. I come up short.

He stares out the window at the ocean, rubbing his thumb almost absentmindedly over the back of my hand. I keep my grip in his, enjoying the touch.

"So," I say eventually. "What happens now?"

His mouth twists as he considers my question.

"Depends," he says.

I blink. "On?"

"On you."

I want to tell him to stop screwing around, but his expression is serious. Patient. Not mocking, this time.

"What about me?"

"The way I see it: I have two options. You can tell me to fuck off, and I'll have to send another pack member to keep an eye on you for the foreseeable future." I shiver, trying to imagine some faceless shifter protector in his place. "Or, I keep guarding you. Protecting you from any demon who comes after you—whether it be Luthor, or someone else. 'Cause he's still out there, and from the sound of it, I don't think he's going to stop."

I raise an eyebrow. "Why would I tell you to fuck off?"

"Who can say?" Kyan smirks. "Maybe you're sick of me."

I catch a trace of doubt underneath the bravado. It emboldens me enough to lean into his chest. His arms come round me.

"You missed the third option," I say lightly.

"Oh, yeah?" He tightens his embrace.

"Yeah. I'm not some helpless damsel." My heart flutters as he shifts his body so he can stare into my eyes. "Maybe we can protect each other. You and me. Together."

"Topaz." Kyan tips up my chin. For the first time, I catch the tiniest hint of blue in the green of his eyes. They are beautiful. So beautiful, no matter what color they are. "I *want* to stay. Not out of some obligation, or duty."

"Then stay." My breath catches as his hand slides into my hair, and he bends to kiss me. When we break apart, I press our foreheads together, breathing him in. *"Stay."*

I gasp as he kisses me again. He tastes like salt; like the ocean. Like freedom.

Two hours later, I am crammed with Ammie into the small breakfast nook overlooking the ocean. Kyan and Sapph are over near the cooktop. Outside, seagulls ride the breeze, and warm sunlight streams through the open windows.

Sapphire slides a sweet-smelling plate of French toast in front of me. "Courtesy of the chef, ma'am."

I look up. From the stove, Kyan shoots me a wink. He has a dishcloth thrown haphazardly over one shoulder, and he's barefoot. The t-shirt he's wearing accentuates the flex of his arms as he returns his attention to the frying pan.

"Hey! Come on, *focus.*"

I blink at the fingers snapping in front of my face. Amethyst rolls her eyes, although a smile twitches at the corners of her mouth.

"As I was *saying,* I've been doing some research, and a magical imbalance is the only thing that could've allowed the Otherworld to spill over into the human world like this." Ammie's brows draw together, and she prods at the food on her plate without taking a bite.

"These rifts opening up all over the place—the hell-hound attacks, and the demons coming after you... all the signs point toward an imbalance. But I'm positive it isn't you, Tee."

"What do you mean?"

"Do you really think the fact that you escaped death all those years ago, could possibly cause all of *this*?"

"Well..." I've been so caught up in the drama and the running and escaping monster attacks, that I haven't really thought about that. *Until now*. "I don't know. I thought so, but now that you mention it..."

"As much as you and Sapph are my world, I think this is far bigger than you, Tee."

Kyan pipes up, then. "She actually has a point, Topaz."

Sapphire nods. All this time, I've been blaming myself, and while I know I've played a role in what is happening, maybe Ammie is right. "Do you think it has anything to do with the Fae Realm?"

"I do," Ammie states firmly. "And, I'm worried."

"Yeah." I swallow back the lump in my throat. "Me too."

If the Fae are in trouble, it is bad news for all species.

"Do you think he's still out there?" Amethyst murmurs. "What happened, Topaz? Really?"

I don't need to ask who she's talking about.

Luthor's final moments, still sharp and fresh, play out yet again in my mind's eye. What stands out above anything else is the rage that warped his inhuman face when I asked why he didn't just take my soul.

"I don't know," I say, my hands twisting together. All of a sudden, I've lost my appetite. "I dared him to take me. And... he didn't. But then he called me an abomination."

"Well, you're not," Amethyst says. "We'll figure this out, okay? Together."

I want to believe the certainty in Amethyst's voice—her unshakable belief that we will find a way forward.

On a day like this, it seems impossible to believe that demons like Luthor are still out there. The sun is high in the sky, and the events of the past week seem like a bad dream.

I wish I could stay here forever, in this home that doesn't even belong to any of us, with nothing but the smell of breakfast, the sound of laughter in the kitchen, and the knowledge of passionate lovemaking with Kyan to come.

A breeze drifts in through the window, stirring my hair. In the distance are dark, rolling clouds, just visible on the horizon. The horrors of the past few days are far from over.

For today, we will eat, and laugh, and pretend everything is all right.

But the horrors are coming.

And only time will tell if we have the courage to face it.

Thank you for reading! I hope you enjoyed *Bewitched in Blood*.

If so, please leave a review at your place of purchase.

MORE IN THE HELLHOUND PROTECTORS SERIES

Bewitched in Dreams (Amethyst's story)

Bewitched in Darkness (Sapphire's story)

Once you've read the *Hellhound Protectors* trilogy, there is a whole new series to enjoy.

The *Blood Fae Chronicles* is set in the same world and features banshee-human hybrid, Maewen and her half-sisters, Aleah and Indigo.

Suggested reading order:

Banshee Cry

Banshee Song

Banshee Power

Banshee Quest: Renna's Curse.

ABOUT THE AUTHOR

Jen Katemi is a *USA Today* bestselling author of steamy contemporary and paranormal fantasy romance. She is published with Evernight Publishing, and previously as Jennifer Lynne with Red Sage. Jen also has forged a successful indie career starting with her popular BLOOD FAE CHRONICLES, GODS OF LOVE and FORBIDDEN series.
When she's not writing, Jen looks after the family, pampers various cats, and tries to find a smidgen of time for her husband. She lives in Melbourne, Australia.
Read more from Jen Katemi and sign up for new release emails at her website:

www.JenKatemi.com